Morton Lichter

TEA AND SYMPATHY

 Random House, New York

Tea and Sympathy

by ROBERT ANDERSON

Photographs by Slim Aarons

This is for

PHYLLIS

whose spirit is everywhere
in this play and in my life.

AUTHOR'S NOTE

I would like to record here my tremendous debt of gratitude to those persons who helped bring *Tea and Sympathy* so glowingly alive on stage.

It is perhaps not a good selling point for a published volume of a play to say that a playwright writes a play for the theater, for the actors, the director, the designer. But he does. And when he is as brilliantly served by these artists as I have been, he feels a miracle has been brought to pass.

It is not often, I think, that a playwright can say of his produced play, this is the way I wanted it. This is the way I dreamed it would be. I *can* say it. And I can say it because of the devotion to this play of so many creative and wonderful people.

R. A.

TEA AND SYMPATHY was first presented by the Playwrights' Company, in association with Mary K. Frank, at the Ethel Barrymore Theatre, New York City, on September 30, 1953, with the following cast:

(IN ORDER OF APPEARANCE)

LAURA REYNOLDS	Deborah Kerr
LILLY SEARS	Florida Friebus
TOM LEE	John Kerr
DAVID HARRIS	Richard Midgley
RALPH	Alan Sues
AL	Dick York
STEVE	Arthur Steuer
BILL REYNOLDS	Leif Erickson
PHIL	Richard Franchot
HERBERT LEE	John McGovern
PAUL	Yale Wexler

Directed by Elia Kazan

Setting and lighting by Jo Mielziner

Clothes designed by Anna Hill Johnstone

SCENES

Act One

A dormitory in a boys' school in New England.
Late afternoon of a day early in June.

Act Two

Scene I. Two days later.
Scene II. Eight-thirty Saturday night.

Act Three

The next afternoon.

ACT ONE

ACT ONE

The scene is a small old Colonial house which is now being used as a dormitory in a boys' school in New England.

On the ground floor at stage right we see the housemaster's study. To stage left is a hall and stairway which leads up to the boys' rooms. At a half-level on stage left is one of the boys' rooms.

The housemaster's study is a warm and friendly room, rather on the dark side, but when the lamps are lighted, there are cheerful pools of light. There is a fireplace in the back wall, bookcases, and upstage right double doors leading to another part of the house. Since there is no common room for the eight boys in this house, there is considerable leniency in letting the boys use the study whenever the door is left ajar.

The boy's bedroom is small, containing a bed, a chair and a bureau. It was meant to be Spartan, but the present occupant has given it a few touches to make it a little more home-like: an Indian print on the bed, India print curtains for the dormer window. There is a phonograph on the ledge of the window. The door to the room is presumed to lead to the sitting room which the roommates share. There is a door from the sitting room which leads to the stair landing. Thus, to get to the bedroom from the stairs, a person must go through the sitting room.

As the curtain rises, it is late afternoon of a day early in June. No lamps have been lighted yet so the study is in a sort of twilight.

Upstairs in his room, TOM LEE *is sitting on his bed playing the guitar and singing softly and casually, the plaintive song, "The Joys of Love" . . .* TOM *is going on eighteen.*

He is young and a little gangling, but intense. He is wearing faded khaki trousers, a white shirt open at the neck and white tennis sneakers.

Seated in the study listening to the singing are LAURA REYNOLDS *and* LILLY SEARS. LAURA *is a lovely, sensitive woman in her mid to late twenties. Her essence is gentleness. She is compassionate and tender. She is wearing a cashmere sweater and a wool skirt. As she listens to* TOM's *singing, she is sewing on what is obviously a period costume.*

LILLY *is in her late thirties, and in contrast to the simple effectiveness of* LAURA's *clothes, she is dressed a little too flashily for her surroundings. . . . It would be in good taste on East 57th Street, but not in a small New England town. . . . A smart suit and hat and a fur piece. As she listens to* TOM *singing, she plays with the martini glass in her hand.*

TOM
(Singing)

The joys of love
Are but a moment long . . .
The pains of love
Endure forever . . .
(*When he has finished, he strums on over the same melody very casually, and hums to it intermittently.*)

LILLY
(*While* TOM *is singing*)

Tom Lee?

4

LAURA

Yes.

LILLY

Doesn't he have an afternoon class?

LAURA

No. He's the only one in the house that doesn't.

LILLY

(When TOM *has finished the song*)
Do you know what he's thinking of?

LAURA

(*Bites off a thread and looks up*)
What do you mean?

LILLY

What all the boys in this school are thinking about. Not only now in the spring, but all the time . . . Sex!
(*She wags her head a little wisely, and smiles.*)

LAURA

Lilly, you just like to shock people.

LILLY

Four hundred boys from the ages of thirteen to nineteen. That's the age, Laura. (*Restless, getting up*) Doesn't it give you the willies sometimes, having all these boys around?

5

LAURA

Of course not. I never think of it that way.

LILLY

Harry tells me they put saltpeter in their food to quiet them down. But the way they look at you, I can't believe it.

LAURA

At me?

LILLY

At any woman worth looking at. When I first came here ten years ago, I didn't think I could stand it. Now I love it. I love watching them look and suffer.

LAURA

Lilly.

LILLY

This is your first spring here, Laura. You wait.

LAURA

They're just boys.

LILLY

The authorities say the ages from thirteen to nineteen . . .

LAURA

Lilly, honestly!

6

LILLY

You sound as though you were in the grave. How old are you?

LAURA

(*Smiling*)

Over twenty-one.

LILLY

They come here ignorant as all get out about women, and then spend the next four years exchanging misinformation. They're so cute, and so damned intense.
(*She shudders again.*)

LAURA

Most of them seem very casual to me.

LILLY

That's just an air they put on. This is the age Romeo should be played. You'd believe him! So intense! These kids would die for love, or almost anything else. Harry says all their themes end in death.

LAURA

That's boys.

LILLY

Failure; death! Dishonor; death! Lose their girls; death! It's gruesome.

7

LAURA

But rather touching too, don't you think?

LILLY

You won't tell your husband the way I was talking?

LAURA

Of course not.

LILLY

Though I don't know why I should care. All the boys talk about me. They have me in and out of bed with every single master in the school—and some married ones, too.

LAURA

(*Kidding her*)

Maybe I'd better listen to them.

LILLY

Oh, never with your husband, of course.

LAURA

Thanks.

LILLY

Even before he met you, Bill never gave me a second glance. He was all the time organizing teams, planning Mountain Club outings.

LAURA

Bill's good at that sort of thing; he likes it.

8

LILLY

And you? (LAURA *looks up at* LILLY *and smiles*) Not a very co-operative witness, are you? I know, mind my own business. But watch out he doesn't drag his usual quota of boys to the lodge in Maine this summer.

LAURA

I've got my own plans for him.
(*She picks up some vacation folders.*)

LILLY

Oh really? What?

LAURA

"Come to Canada" . . . I want to get him off on a trip alone.

LILLY

I don't blame you.

LAURA

(*Reflecting*)
Of course I'd really like to go back to Italy. We had a good time there last summer. It was wonderful then. You should have seen Bill.

LILLY

Look, honey, you married Bill last year on his sabbatical leave, and abroad to boot. Teachers on sabbatical leave abroad are like men in uniform during the war. They never look so good again.

9

LAURA

Bill looks all right to me.

LILLY

Did Bill ever tell you about the party we gave him before his sabbatical?

LAURA

Yes. I have a souvenir from it.
> (*She is wearing a rather large Woolworth's diamond ring on a gold chain around her neck . . . She now pulls it out from her sweater.*)

LILLY

I never thought he'd use that Five-and-Dime engagement ring we gave him that night. Even though we gave him an awful ribbing, we all expected him to come back a bachelor.

LAURA

You make it sound as though you kidded him into marrying.

LILLY

Oh, no, honey, it wasn't that.

LAURA
> (*With meaning*)

No, it wasn't.
> (LAURA *laughs at* LILLY.)

LILLY

Well, I've got to go. You know, Bill could have married any number of the right kind of girls around here. But I knew it would take more than the right kind of girl to get Bill to marry. It would take something special. And you're something special.

LAURA

How should I take that?

LILLY

As a compliment. Thanks for the drink. Don't tell Harry I had one when you see him at dinner.

LAURA

We won't be over to the hall. I've laid in a sort of feast for tonight.

LILLY

Celebrating something?

LAURA

No, just an impulse.

LILLY

Well, don't tell Harry anyway.

LAURA

You'd better stop talking the way you've been talking, or I won't have to tell him.

11

LILLY

Now, look, honey, don't you start going puritan on me. You're the only one in this school I can shoot my mouth off to, so don't change, baby. Don't change.

LAURA

I won't.

LILLY

Some day I'm going to wheedle out of you all the juicy stories you must have from when you were in the theater.

LAURA

Lilly, you would make the most hardened chorus girl blush.

LILLY

(*Pleased*)

Really?

LAURA

Really.

LILLY

That's the sweetest thing you've said to me in days. Good-bye.

(*She goes out the door, and a moment later we hear the outside door close.*)

LAURA

(*Sits for a moment, listening to* TOM's *rather plaintive whistling. She rises and looks at the Canada vacation literature*

on the desk, and then, looking at her watch, goes to the door,
opens it, and calls up the stairway)

Tom ... Oh, Tom.

(The moment TOM *hears his name, he jumps from the*
bed, and goes through the sitting room, and appears
on the stairs.)

TOM

Yes?

LAURA

(She is very friendly with him, comradely)
If it won't spoil your supper, come on down for a cup of tea.

*(*TOM *goes back into his room and brushes his hair,*
then he comes on down the stairs, and enters the study.
He enters this room as though it were something rare
and special. This is where LAURA *lives.)*

LAURA

(Has gone out to the other part of the house. Comes to door-
way for a moment pouring cream from bottle to pitcher)
I've just about finished your costume for the play, and we
can have a fitting.

TOM

Sure. That'd be great. Do you want the door open or shut?

LAURA

(Goes off again)
It doesn't make any difference. (TOM *shuts the door. He is*
deeply in love with this woman, though he knows nothing

13

can come of it. It is a sort of delayed puppy love. It is very touching and very intense. They are easy with each other, casual, though he is always trying in thinly veiled ways to tell her he loves her. LAURA *enters with tea tray and sees him closing the door. She puts tray on table)* Perhaps you'd better leave it ajar, so that if some of the other boys get out of class early, they can come in too.

TOM

(Is disappointed)

Oh, sure.

LAURA

(Goes off for the plate of cookies, but pauses long enough to watch TOM *open the door the merest crack. She is amused. In a moment, she re-enters with a plate of cookies)*

Help yourself.

TOM

Thanks.

(He takes a cookie, and then sits on the floor, near her chair.)

LAURA

Are the boys warm enough in the rooms? They shut down the heat so early this spring, I guess they didn't expect this little chill.

TOM

We're fine. But this in nice.

(He indicates low fire in fireplace.)

LAURA

(*Goes back to her sewing*)

I heard you singing.

TOM

I'm sorry if it bothered you.

LAURA

It was very nice.

TOM

If it ever bothers you, just bang on the radiator.

LAURA

What was the name of the song? It's lovely.

TOM

It's an old French song ... "The Joys of Love" ...
    (*He speaks the lyric*)
The joys of love
Are but a moment long,
The pain of love
Endures forever.

LAURA

And is that true? (TOM *shrugs his shoulders*) You sang as
though you knew all about the pains of love.

TOM

And you don't think I do?

15

LAURA

Well . . .

TOM

You're right.

LAURA

Only the joys.

TOM

Neither, really.
(Teapot whistles off stage.)

LAURA

Then you're a fake. Listening to you, one would think you knew everything there was to know. (*Rises and goes to next room for tea*) Anyway, I don't believe it. A boy like you.

TOM

It's true.

LAURA

(Off stage)
Aren't you bringing someone to the dance after the play Saturday?

TOM

Yes.

LAURA

Well, there.

TOM

You.

LAURA

(*Reappears in doorway with teapot*)
Me?

TOM

Yes, you're going to be a hostess, aren't you?

LAURA

Yes, of course, but . . .

TOM

As a member of the committee, I'm taking you. All the
committee drew lots . . .

LAURA

And you lost.

TOM

I won.

LAURA

(*A little embarrassed by this*)
Oh. My husband could have taken me.
(*She sits down again in her chair.*)

TOM

He's not going to be in town. Don't you remember, Mountain Climbing Club has its final outing this week-end.

17

LAURA

Oh, yes, of course. I'd forgotten.

TOM

He's out a lot on that kind of thing, isn't he? (LAURA *ignores his probing*) I hope you're not sorry that I'm to be your escort.

LAURA

Why, I'll be honored.

TOM

I'm supposed to find out tactfully and without your knowing it what color dress you'll be wearing.

LAURA

Why?

TOM

The committee will send you a corsage.

LAURA

Oh, how nice. Well, I don't have much to choose from, I guess my yellow.

TOM

The boy who's in charge of getting the flowers thinks a corsage should be something like a funeral decoration. So I'm taking personal charge of getting yours.

LAURA

Thank you.

TOM

You must have gotten lots of flowers when you were acting in the theater.

LAURA

Oh, now and then. Nothing spectacular.

TOM

I can't understand how a person would give up the theater to come and live in a school . . . I'm sorry. I mean, I'm glad you did, but, well . . .

LAURA

If you knew the statistics on unemployed actors, you might understand. Anyway, I was never any great shakes at it.

TOM

I can't believe that.

LAURA

Then take my word for it.

TOM

(*After a moment, looking into the fire, pretending to be casual, but actually touching on his love for* LAURA)
Did you ever do any of Shaw's plays?

LAURA

Yes.

19

TOM

We got an assignment to read any Shaw play we wanted.
I picked *Candida*.

LAURA

Because it was the shortest?

TOM

(*Laughs*)
No . . . because it sounded like the one I'd like the best, one
I could understand. Did you ever play Candida?

LAURA

In stock—a very small stock company, way up in Northern
Vermont.

TOM

Do you think she did right to send Marchbanks away?

LAURA

Well, Shaw made it seem right. Don't you think?

TOM

(*Really talking about himself*)
That Marchbanks sure sounded off a lot. I could never
sound off like that, even if I loved a woman the way he did.
She could have made him seem awfully small if she'd wanted
to.

LAURA

Well, I guess she wasn't that kind of woman. Now stand up. Let's see if this fits.

(*She rises with dress in her hands.*)

TOM

(*Gets up*)

My Dad's going to hit the roof when he hears I'm playing another girl.

LAURA

I think you're a good sport not to mind. Besides, it's a good part. Lady Teazle in *The School For Scandal.*

TOM

(*Puts on top of dress*)

It all started when I did Lady Macbeth last year. You weren't here yet for that. Lucky you.

LAURA

I hear it was very good.

TOM

You should have read a letter I got from my father. They printed a picture of me in the *Alumni Bulletin,* in costume. He was plenty peeved about it.

LAURA

He shouldn't have been.

21

TOM

He wrote me saying he might be up here today on Alumni Fund business. If he comes over here, and you see him, don't tell him about this.

LAURA

I won't . . . What about your mother? Did she come up for the play?
(*She helps him button the dress.*)

TOM

I don't see my mother. Didn't you know?
(*He starts to roll up pants legs.*)

LAURA

Why no. I didn't.

TOM

She and my father are divorced.

LAURA

I'm sorry.

TOM

You needn't be. They aren't. I was supposed to hold them together. That was how I happened to come into the world. I didn't work. That's a terrible thing, you know, to make a flop of the first job you've got in life.

LAURA

Don't you ever see her?

TOM

Not since I was five. I was with her till five, and then my father took me away. All I remember about my mother is that she was always telling me to go outside and bounce a ball.

LAURA

(*Handing him skirt of the dress*)
You must have done something before Lady Macbeth. When did you play that character named Grace?

TOM

(*Stiffens*)
I never played anyone called Grace.

LAURA

But I hear the boys sometimes calling you Grace. I thought . . . (*She notices that he's uncomfortable*) I'm sorry. Have I said something terrible?

TOM

No.

LAURA

But I have. I'm sorry.

TOM

It's all right. But it's a long story. Last year over at the movies, they did a revival of Grace Moore in *One Night of Love*. I'd seen the revival before the picture came. And I

guess I oversold it, or something. But she was wonderful!
. . . Anyway, some of the guys started calling me Grace. It
was my own fault, I guess.

LAURA

Nicknames can be terrible. I remember at one time I was
called "Beany." I can't remember why, now, but I remember
it made me mad. (*She adjusts the dress a little*) Hold still a
moment. We'll have to let this out around here. (*She indicates
the bosom*) What size do you want to be?

TOM

(*He is embarrassed, but rather nicely, not obviously and
farcically. In his embarrassment he looks at* LAURA'S *bosom,
then quickly away*)
I don't know. Whatever you think.

LAURA

(*She indicates he is to stand on a small wooden footstool*)
I should think you would have invited some girl up to see
you act, and then take her to the dance.

TOM

(*Gets on stool*)
There's nobody I could ask.

LAURA

(*Working on hem of dress*)
What do you mean?

TOM

I don't know any girls, really.

24

LAURA

Oh, certainly back home . . .

TOM

Last ten years I haven't been home, I mean really home.
Summers my father packs me off to camps, and the rest of
the time I've been at boarding schools.

LAURA

What about Christmas vacation, and Easter?

TOM

My father gets a raft of tickets to plays and concerts, and
sends me and my aunt.

LAURA

I see.

TOM

So I mean it when I say I don't know any girls.

LAURA

Your roommate, Al, knows a lot of girls. Why not ask him
to fix you up with a blind date?

TOM

I don't know . . . I can't even dance. I'm telling you this so
you won't expect anything of me Saturday night.

LAURA

We'll sit out and talk.

TOM

Okay.

LAURA

Or I could teach you how to dance. It's quite simple.

TOM
(*Flustered*)

You?

LAURA

Why not?

TOM

I mean, isn't a person supposed to go to some sort of dancing class or something?
(*He gets down from footstool.*)

LAURA

Not necessarily. Look, I'll show you how simple it is. (*She assumes the dancing position*) Hold your left hand out this way, and put your right hand around my—(*She stops, as she sees him looking at her*) Oh, now you're kidding me. A boy your age and you don't know how to dance.

TOM

I'm not kidding you.

LAURA

Well, then, come on. I had to teach my husband. Put your arm around me.

(*She raises her arms.*)

TOM

(*Looks at her a moment, afraid to touch this woman he loves.
Then to pass it off*)

We better put it off. We'd look kind of silly, both of us in skirts.

LAURA

All right. Take it off, then. No, wait a minute. Just let me stand off and take a look . . . (*She walks around him*) You're going to make a very lovely girl.

TOM

Thank you, ma'am . . .

(*He kids a curtsy, like a girl, and starts out of his costume.* MR. HARRIS, *a good-looking young master, comes in the hallway and starts up to Tom's room. On the landing, he knocks on Tom's door.*)

LAURA

I wonder who that is?

TOM

All the other fellows have late afternoon classes.

TEA AND SYMPATHY

LAURA

(Opens the door wider, and looks up the stairs)
Yes? Oh, David.

HARRIS

(Turns and looks down the stairs)
Oh, hello, Laura.

LAURA

I just was wondering who was coming in.
(TOM proceeds to get out of the costume.)

HARRIS

I want to see Tom Lee.

LAURA

He's down here. I'm making his costume for the play.

HARRIS

I wonder if I could see him for a moment?

LAURA

Why yes, of course. Tom, Mr. Harris would like to see you.
Do you want to use our study, David? I can go into the living
room.

HARRIS

No, thanks. I'll wait for him in his room. Will you ask him
to come up?
(He opens the door and goes in.)

LAURA

(*Is puzzled at his intensity, the urgency in his voice. Comes back in the study*)
Tom, Mr. Harris would like to see you in your room. He's gone along.

TOM

That's funny.

LAURA

Wait a minute . . . take this up with you, try it on in front of your mirror . . . see if you can move in it . . . (*She hands him skirt of costume*) When Mr. Harris is through, bring the costume back.

TOM

(*Anxious over what* HARRIS *wants to see him about*)
Yeah, sure. (*He starts out, then stops and picks up a cookie. He looks at her lovingly*) Thanks for tea.

LAURA

You're welcome.
(TOM *goes to the door as* LAURA *turns to the desk. He stands in the door a moment and looks at her back, then he turns and shuts the door and heads upstairs.* HARRIS *has come into* TOM's *bedroom, and is standing there nervously clenching and unclenching his hands.*)

TOM

(*Off stage, presumably in the study he shares with his roommate*)

Mr. Harris?
> (LAURA *wanders off into the other part of the house after looking for a moment at the Canada vacation material on the desk.*)

HARRIS

I'm in here.

TOM

> (*Comes in a little hesitantly*)

Oh. Hello, sir.
> (HARRIS *closes the door to the bedroom.* TOM *regards this action with some nervousness.*)

HARRIS

Well?

TOM

> (*Has dumped some clothes from a chair to his bed. Offers chair to* HARRIS)

Sir?

HARRIS

What did you tell the Dean?

TOM

What do you mean, Mr. Harris?

HARRIS

What did you tell the Dean?

TOM

When? What are you talking about, sir?

HARRIS

Didn't the Dean call you in?

TOM

No. Why should he?

HARRIS

He didn't call you in and ask you about last Saturday after-noon?

TOM

Why should he? I didn't do anything wrong.

HARRIS

About being with me?

TOM

I'm allowed to leave town for the day in the company of a master.

HARRIS

I don't believe you. You must have said something.

TOM

About what?

HARRIS

About you and me going down to the dunes and swimming.

TOM

Why should I tell him about that?

HARRIS

(*Threatening*)
Why didn't you keep your mouth shut?

TOM

About what? What, for God's sake?

HARRIS

I never touched you, did I?

TOM

What do you mean, touch me?

HARRIS

Did you say to the Dean I touched you?

TOM

(*Turning away from* HARRIS)
I don't know what you're talking about.

HARRIS

Here's what I'm talking about. The Dean's had me on the carpet all afternoon. I probably won't be reappointed next year . . . and all because I took you swimming down off the dunes on Saturday.

TOM

Why should he have you on the carpet for that?

HARRIS

You can't imagine, I suppose.

TOM

What did you do wrong?

HARRIS

Nothing! Nothing, unless you made it seem like something wrong. Did you?

TOM

I told you I didn't see the Dean.

HARRIS

You will. He'll call for you. Bunch of gossiping old busy-bodies! Well . . . (*He starts for the door, stops, turns around and softens. He comes back to the puzzled* TOM) I'm sorry . . . It probably wasn't your fault. It was my fault. I should have been more . . . discreet . . . Good-bye. Good luck with your music.

(TOM *hasn't understood. He doesn't know what to say. He makes a helpless gesture with his hands.* HARRIS *goes into the other room on his way out. Three boys, about seventeen, come in from the downstairs hall*

33

door and start up the stairs. They're carrying books.
All are wearing sports jackets, khaki or flannel trousers,
white or saddle rubber-soled shoes.)

AL

I don't believe a word of it.

RALPH

(He is large and a loud-mouthed bully)
I'm telling you the guys saw them down at the dunes.

AL

(He is TOM's *roommate, an athlete)*
So what?

RALPH

They were bare-assed.

AL

Shut up, will you? You want Mrs. Reynolds to hear you?

RALPH

Okay. You watch and see. Harris'll get bounced, and I'm
gonna lock my room at night as long as Tom is living in this
house.

AL

Oh, dry up!

RALPH

Jeeze, you're his roommate and you're not worried.

34

HARRIS

(Comes out the door and starts down the stairs)
Hello.
(He goes down stairs and out.)

AL

Sir.

RALPH

Do you believe me now? You aren't safe. Believe me.

STEVE

*(He is small, RALPH's appreciative audience. He comes in the
front door)*
Hey, Al, can I come in watch Mrs. Morrison nurse her kid?

RALPH

You're the loudest-mouthed bastard I ever heard. You want
to give it away.

STEVE

It's time. How about it, Al?

AL

(Grudgingly)
Come on.
*(TOM hears them coming, and moves to bolt his door,
but STEVE and RALPH break in before he gets to the
door. He watches them from the doorway. STEVE
rushes to the bed and throws himself across it, looking*

35

out the window next to the bed. RALPH *settles down next to him.)*

AL
(*To* TOM *as he comes in*)
Hi. These horny bastards.

STEVE
Al, bring the glasses.
(AL *goes into sitting room.*)

RALPH
Some day she's going to wean that little bastard and spoil all our fun.

STEVE
Imagine sitting in a window . . .

TOM
(*Has been watching this with growing annoyance*)
Will you guys get out of here?

RALPH
(*Notices* TOM *for the first time*)
What's the matter with you, Grace?

TOM
This is my damned room.

RALPH
Gracie's getting private all of a sudden.

TOM

I don't want a lot of Peeping Toms lying on my bed watching a . . . a . . .

STEVE

You want it all for yourself, don't you?

RALPH

Or aren't you interested in women?

AL

(*Comes back in with field glasses*)
Shut up! (*Looks out window, then realizes* TOM *is watching him. Embarrassed*) These horny bastards.

STEVE

(*Looking*)

Geeze!

RALPH

(*A bully, riding down on* TOM)
I thought you were going to play ball with us Saturday.

TOM

I didn't feel like it.

RALPH

What *did* you feel like doing, huh?

AL

Will you shut up?

37

STEVE

Hey, lookit.
(*Grabs glasses from* AL. AL *leaves room.*)

TOM

(*Climbing over* STEVE *and* RALPH *and trying to pull the shade*)
I told you to get out. I told you last time . . .

RALPH

(*Grabbing hold of* TOM, *and holding him down*)
Be still, boy, or she'll see, and you'll spoil everything.

TOM

Horny bastard. Get out of here.

RALPH

Who are you calling a horny bastard? (*He grabs hold of*
TOM *more forcefully, and slaps him a couple of times across
the face, not trying to hurt him, but just to humiliate him.*
STEVE *gets in a few pokes and in a moment, it's not in fun, but
verging on the serious*) You don't mean that now, boy, do
you . . . Do you, Grace? (*He slaps him again.*)

AL

(*Hearing the scuffle, comes in and hauls* RALPH *and* STEVE *off*
TOM)
Come on, come on, break it up. Clear out.
(*He has them both standing up now,* TOM *still on the
bed.*)

RALPH

I just don't like that son of a bitch calling me a horny bastard. Maybe if it was Dr. Morrison instead of Mrs. Morrison, he'd be more interested. Hey, wouldn't you, Grace?

(*He tries to stick his face in front of* TOM, *but* AL *holds him back.*)

AL

Come on, lay off the guy, will you? Go on. Get ready for supper.

(*He herds them out during this. When they have left the room,* TOM *gets up and goes to bureau and gets a handkerchief. He has a bloody nose. He lies down on the bed, his head tilted back to stop the blood.*)

AL

(*In doorway*)

You all right?

TOM

Yeah.

(RALPH *and* STEVE *go up the stairway singing in raucous voices, "One Night of Love." The downstairs outside door opens, and* BILL REYNOLDS *enters the hall with a student,* PHIL. BILL *is* LAURA's *husband. He is large and strong with a tendency to be gruff. He's wearing gray flannel trousers, a tweed jacket, a blue button-down shirt. He is around forty.*)

BILL

Okay, boy, we'll look forward to—(*He notices* RALPH *still singing. He goes to the bend in the stairs and calls*) Hey, Ralph. . . . Ralph!

RALPH

(*Stops singing up out of sight*)
You calling me, Mr. Reynolds, sir?

BILL

Yeah. Keep it down to a shout, will you?

RALPH

Oh, *yes, sir.* Sorry, I didn't know I was disturbing you, Mr. Reynolds.

BILL

(*Comes back and talks with* PHIL *at the bend in the stairway*)
Phil, you come on up to the lodge around . . . Let's see . . . We'll open the lodge around July first, so you plan to come up say, July third, and stay for two weeks. Okay?

PHIL

That'll be swell, sir.

BILL

Frank Hocktor's coming then. You get along with Frank, don't you? He's a regular guy.

PHIL

Oh, sure.

BILL

The float's all gone to pieces. We can make that your project to fix it up. Okay?

PHIL

Thanks a lot, Mr. Reynolds.
(*He goes on up the stairs.*)

BILL

See you.
(*He comes in and crosses to phone and starts to call.*)

LAURA
(*Off stage*)

Tom?
(BILL *looks around in the direction of the voice, but says nothing.*)

LAURA
(*Comes on*)

Oh, Bill. Tom was down trying on his costume. I thought
... You're early.

BILL

Yes. I want to catch the Dean before he leaves his office.
(LAURA *goes up to him to be kissed, but he's too intent on the phone, and she compromises by kissing his cheek*) Hello, this is Mr. Reynolds. Is the Dean still in his office?

LAURA

What's the matter, Bill?

41

BILL

Nothing very pretty. Oh? How long ago? All right. Thanks. I'll give him a couple of minutes, then I'll call him home. (*Hangs up*) Well, they finally caught up with Harris. (*He goes into the next room to take off his jacket.*)

LAURA

What do you mean, "caught up" with him?

BILL

(*Off stage*)
You're going to hear it anyhow . . . so . . . last Saturday they caught him down in the dunes, naked.

LAURA

(*Crosses to close door to hall*)
What's wrong with that?

BILL

(*Enters and crosses to fireplace and starts to go through letters propped there. He has taken off his jacket*)
He wasn't alone.

LAURA

Oh.

BILL

He was lying there naked in the dunes, and one of the students was lying there naked too. Just to talk about it is disgusting.

42

LAURA

I see.

BILL

I guess you'll admit that's something.

LAURA

I can't see that it's necessarily conclusive.

BILL

With a man like Harris, it's conclusive enough. (*Then casually*) The student with him was—

LAURA

(*Interrupting*)
I'm not sure I care to know.

BILL

I'm afraid you're going to have to know sooner or later, Laura. It was Tom Lee.
(TOM *rises from bed, grabs a towel and goes out up the stairs.* LAURA *just looks at* BILL *and frowns.*)

BILL

Some of the boys down on the Varsity Club outing came on them . . . or at least saw them . . . And Fin Hadley saw them too, and he apparently used his brains for once and spoke to the Dean.

LAURA

And?

43

BILL

He's had Harris on the carpet this afternoon. I guess he'll
be fired. I certainly hope so. Maybe Tom too, I don't know.

LAURA

They put two and two together?

BILL

Yes, Laura.

LAURA

I suppose this is all over school by now.

BILL

I'm afraid so.

LAURA

And most of the boys know.

BILL

Yes.

LAURA

So what's going to happen to Tom?

BILL

(*Takes pipe from mantelpiece and cleans it*)
I know you won't like this, Laura, but I think he should be
kicked out. I think you've got to let people know the school

doesn't stand for even a hint of this sort of thing. He should be booted.

LAURA

For what?

BILL

Look, a boy's caught coming out of Ellie Martin's rooms across the river. That's enough evidence. Nobody asks particulars. They don't go to Ellie's rooms to play Canasta. It's the same here.

LAURA

(*Hardly daring to suggest it*)
But, Bill . . . you don't think . . . I mean, you don't think Tom is . . . (*She stops.* BILL *looks at her a moment, his answer is in his silence*) Oh, Bill!

BILL

And I'm ashamed and sorry as hell for his father. Herb Lee was always damned good to me . . . came down from college when I was playing football here . . . helped me get into college . . . looked after me when I was in college and he was in law school . . . And I know he put the boy in my house hoping I could do something with him.
(*He dials number.*)

LAURA

And you feel you've failed.

45

BILL

Yes. (*He pauses*) With your help, I might say.
(*Busy signal. He hangs up.*)

LAURA

How?

BILL

Because, Laura, the boy would rather sit around here and talk with you and listen to music and strum his guitar.

LAURA

Bill, I'm not to blame for everything. Everything's not my fault.

BILL

(*Disregarding this*)
What a lousy thing for Herb. (*He looks at a small picture of a team on his desk*) That's Herb. He was Graduate Manager of the team when I was a sophomore in college. He was always the manager of the teams, and he really wanted his son to be there in the center of the picture.

LAURA

Why are you calling the Dean?

BILL

I'm going to find out what's being done.

46

LAURA

I've never seen you like this before.

BILL

This is something that touches me very closely. The name of the school, its reputation, the reputation of all of us here. I went here and my father before me, and one day I hope our children will come here, when we have them. And, of course, one day I hope to be headmaster.

LAURA

Let's assume that you're right about Harris. It's a terrible thing to say on the evidence you've got, but let's assume you're right. Does it necessarily follow that Tom—

BILL

Tom was his friend. Everyone knew that.

LAURA

Harris encouraged him in his music.

BILL

Come on, Laura.

LAURA

What if Tom's roommate, Al, or some other great big athlete had been out with Harris?

BILL

He wouldn't have been.

LAURA

I'm saying what if he had been? Would you have jumped
to the same conclusion?

BILL

It would have been different. Tom's always been an off-
horse. And now it's quite obvious why. If he's kicked out,
maybe it'll bring him to his senses. But he won't change if
nothing's done about it. (LAURA *turns away.* BILL *starts to look
over his mail again*) Anyway, why are you so concerned over
what happens to Tom Lee?

LAURA

I've come to know him. You even imply that I am some-
what responsible for his present reputation.

BILL

All right. I shouldn't have said that. But you watch, now
that it's out in the open. Look at the way he walks, the way
he sometimes stands.

LAURA

Oh, Bill!

BILL

All right, so a woman doesn't notice these things. But a
man knows a queer when he sees one. (*He has opened a letter.
Reads*) The bookstore now has the book you wanted . . .
The Rose and The Thorn. What's that?

LAURA

A book of poems. Do you know, Bill, I'll bet he doesn't even know the meaning of the word . . . queer.

BILL

What do you think he is?

LAURA

I think he's a nice sensitive kid who doesn't know the meaning of the word.

BILL

He's eighteen, or almost. I don't know.

LAURA

How much did you know at eighteen?

BILL

A lot. (*At the desk he now notices the Canada literature*) What are these?

LAURA

What?

BILL

These.

LAURA

Oh, nothing.

BILL

(*He throws them in wastebasket, then notices her look*)
Well, they're obviously something.
(*He takes them out of wastebasket.*)

LAURA

(*The joy of it gone for her*)
I was thinking we might take a motor trip up there this
summer.

BILL

(*Dialing phone again*)
I wish you'd said something about it earlier. I've already
invited some of the scholarship boys up to the lodge. I can't
disappoint them.

LAURA

Of course not.

BILL

If you'd said something earlier.

LAURA

It's my fault.

BILL

It's nobody's fault, it's just—Hello, Fitz, Bill Reynolds—
I was wondering if you're going to be in tonight after supper
... Oh ... oh, I see ... Supper? Well, sure I could talk about

it at supper. . . . Well, no, I think I'd better drop over alone.
. . . All right. I'll see you at the house then . . . Good-bye.

(LAURA *looks at him, trying to understand him.* BILL *comes to her to speak softly to her. Seeing him come, she holds out her arms to be embraced, but he just takes her chin in his hand.*)

BILL

Look, Laura, when I brought you here a year ago, I told you it was a tough place for a woman with a heart like yours. I told you you'd run across boys, big and little boys, full of problems, problems which for the moment seem gigantic and heartbreaking. And you promised me then you wouldn't get all taken up with them. Remember?

LAURA

Yes.

BILL

When I was a kid in school here, I had my problems too. There's a place up by the golf course where I used to go off alone Sunday afternoons and cry my eyes out. I used to lie on my bed just the way Tom does, listening to phonograph records hour after hour. (LAURA, *touched by this, kneels at his side*) But I got over it, Laura. I learned how to take it. (LAURA *looks at him. This touches her*) When the headmaster's wife gave you this teapot, she told you what she tells all the new masters' wives. You have to be an interested bystander.

LAURA

I know.

BILL

Just as she said, all you're supposed to do is every once in a while give the boys a little tea and sympathy. Do you remember?

LAURA

Yes, I remember. It's just that . . .

BILL

What?

LAURA

This age—seventeen, eighteen—it's so . . .

BILL

I know.

LAURA

John was this age when I married him.

BILL

Look, Laura . . .

LAURA

I know. You don't like me to talk about John, but . . .

BILL

It's not that. It's . . .

LAURA

He was just this age, eighteen or so, when I married him.
We both were. And I know now how this age can suffer. It's
a heartbreaking time . . . no longer a boy . . . not yet a man
. . . Bill? Bill?

BILL

(*Looks at her awkwardly a moment, then starts to move off*)
I'd better clean up if I'm going to get to the Dean's for
supper. You don't mind, do you?

LAURA

(*Very quietly*)
I got things in for dinner here. But they'll keep.

BILL

(*Awkwardly*)
I'm sorry, Laura. But you understand, don't you? About
this business? (LAURA *shakes her head,* "No." BILL *stands over
her, a little put out that she has not understood his reasoning.
He starts to say something several times, then stops. Finally
he notices the Five-and-Dime engagement ring around her
neck. He touches it*) You're not going to wear this thing to
the dining hall, are you?

LAURA

Why not?

BILL

It was just a gag. It means something to you, but to them . . .

53

LAURA

(Bearing in, but gently)
Does it mean anything to you, Bill?

BILL

Well, it did, but . . .
(He stops with a gesture, unwilling to go into it all.)

LAURA

I think you're ashamed of the night you gave it to me. That you ever let me see you needed help. That night in Italy, in some vague way you cried out . . .

BILL

What is the matter with you today? *Me* crying out for help.
(He heads for the other room. A knock on study door is heard.)

BILL

It's probably Tom.
(LAURA goes to door.)

HERB

(This is HERBERT LEE, TOM's father. He is a middle-sized man, fancying himself a man of the world and an extrovert. He is dressed as a conservative Boston businessman, but with still a touch of the collegiate in his attire—button-down shirt, etc.)
Mrs. Reynolds?

LAURA

Yes?

54

BILL

(*Stopped by the voice, turns*)
Herb! Come in.

HERB

(*Coming in*)
Hiya, Bill. How are you, fella?

BILL

(*Taking his hand*)
I'm fine, Herb.

HERB

(*Poking his finger into* BILL'*s chest*)
Great to see you. (*Looks around to* LAURA) Oh, uh . . .

BILL

I don't think you've met Laura, Herb. This is Laura. Laura, this is Herb Lee, Tom's father.

HERB

(*Hearty and friendly, meant to put people at their ease*)
Hello, Laura.

LAURA

I've heard so much about you.

HERB

(*After looking at her for a moment*)
I like her, Bill. I like her very much. (LAURA *blushes, and is a little taken aback by this. To* LAURA) What I'd like to

55

know is how did you manage to do it? (*Cuffing* BILL) I'll bet you make her life miserable ... You look good, Bill.

BILL

You don't look so bad yourself.
(*He takes in a notch in his belt.*)

HERB

No, *you're* in shape. I never had anything to keep in shape, but you ... You should have seen this boy, Laura.

LAURA

I've seen pictures.

HERB

Only exercise I get these days is bending the elbow.

LAURA

May I get you something? A drink?

HERB

No, thanks. I haven't got much time.

BILL

You drive out from Boston, Herb?

HERB

No, train. You know, Bill, I think that's the same old train you and I used to ride in when we came here.

BILL

Probably is.

HERB

If I don't catch the six-fifty-four, I'll have to stay all night,
and I'd rather not.

BILL

We'd be glad to put you up.

HERB

No. You're putting me up in a couple of weeks at the reunion. That's imposing enough. (*There is an awkward pause.
Both men sit down*) I . . . uh . . . was over at the Dean's this
afternoon.

BILL

Oh, he called you?

HERB

Why, no. I was up discussing Alumni Fund matters with
him . . . and . . . Do you know about it?

BILL

You mean about Tom?

HERB

Yes.
    (*Looks at* LAURA.)

BILL

Laura knows too.

(*He reaches for her to come to him, and he puts his arm around her waist.*)

HERB

Well, after we discussed the Fund, he told me about that. Thought I ought to hear about it from him. Pretty casual about it, I thought.

BILL

Well, that's Fitz.

HERB

What I want to know is, what was a guy like Harris doing at the school?

BILL

I tried to tell them.

HERB

Was there anyone around like that in our day, Bill?

BILL

No. You're right.

HERB

I tried to find the guy. I wanted to punch his face for him. But he's cleared out. Is Tom around?

LAURA

He's in his room.

HERB

How'd he get mixed up with a guy like that?

BILL

I don't know, Herb ...

HERB

I know. I shouldn't ask you. I know. Of course I don't believe Tom was really involved with this fellow. If I believed
that, I'd ... well, I don't know what I'd do. You don't believe
it, do you, Bill?

BILL

Why ...
(*Looks at* LAURA.)

HERB

(*Cutting in*)
Of course you don't. But what's the matter? What's happened, Bill? Why isn't my boy a regular fellow? He's had
every chance to be since he was knee-high to a grasshopper
—boys' camps every summer, boarding schools. What do you
think, Laura?

LAURA

I'm afraid I'm not the one to ask, Mr. Lee.
(*She breaks away from* BILL.)

HERB

He's always been with men and boys. Why doesn't some of it rub off?

LAURA

You see, I feel he's a "regular fellow" . . . whatever that is.

HERB

You do?

LAURA

If it's sports that matter, he's an excellent tennis player.

HERB

But Laura, he doesn't even play tennis like a regular fellow. No hard drives and cannon-ball serves. He's a cut artist. He can put more damn twists on that ball.

LAURA

He wins. He's the school champion. And isn't he the champion of your club back home?
(TOM *comes down the stairs and enters his bedroom with the costume skirt and towel.*)

HERB

I'm glad you mentioned that . . . because that's just what I mean. Do you know, Laura, his winning that championship brought me one of my greatest humiliations? I hadn't been able to watch the match. I was supposed to be in from a round of golf in time, but we got held up on every hole . . .

60

And when I got back to the locker room, I heard a couple of men talking about Tom's match in the next locker section. And what they said, cut me to the quick, Laura. One of them said, "It's a damn shame Tom Lee won the match. He's a good player, all right, but John Batty is such a regular guy." John Batty was his opponent. Now what pleasure was there for me in that?

BILL

I know what you mean.

HERB

I *want* to be proud of him. My God, that's why I had him in the first place. That's why I took him from his mother when we split up, but . . . Look, this is a terrible thing to say, but you know the scholarships the University Club sponsors for needy kids . . .

BILL

Sure.

HERB

Well, I contribute pretty heavily to it, and I happened to latch on to one of the kids we help—an orphan. I sort of talk to him like a father, go up to see him at his school once in a while, and that kid listens to me . . . and you know what, he's shaping up better than my own son.

(*There is an awkward pause. Upstairs* TOM *has put a record on the phonograph. It starts playing now.*)

BILL

You saw the Dean, Herb?

HERB

Yes.

BILL

And?

HERB

He told me the circumstances. Told me he was confident that Tom was innocently involved. He actually apologized for the whole thing. He did say that some of the faculty had suggested—though he didn't go along with this—that Tom would be more comfortable if I took him out of school. But I'm not going to. He's had nothing but comfort all his life, and look what's happened. My associates ask me what he wants to be, and I tell them he hasn't made up his mind. Because I'll be damned if I'll tell them he wants to be a singer of folk songs.

(TOM *lies on the bed listening to the music.*)

BILL

So you're going to leave him in?

HERB

Of course. Let him stick it out. It'll be a good lesson.

LAURA

Mightn't it be more than just a lesson, Mr. Lee?

62

HERB

Oh, he'll take some kidding. He'll have to work extra hard to prove to them he's . . . well, manly. It may be the thing that brings him to his senses.

LAURA

Mr. Lee, Tom's a very sensitive boy. He's a very lonely boy.

HERB

Why should he be lonely? I've always seen to it that he's been with people . . . at camps, at boarding schools.

BILL

He's certainly an off-horse, Herb.

HERB

That's a good way of putting it, Bill. An off-horse. Well, he's going to have to learn to run with the other horses. Well, I'd better be going up.

LAURA

Mr. Lee, this may sound terribly naive of me, and perhaps a trifle indelicate, but I don't believe your son knows what this is all about. Why Mr. Harris was fired, why the boys will kid him.

HERB

You mean . . .
(*Stops.*)

63

LAURA

I'm only guessing. But I think when it comes to these boys, we often take too much knowledge for granted. And I think it's going to come as a terrible shock when he finds out what they're talking about. Not just a lesson, a shock.

HERB

I don't believe he's as naive as all that. I just don't. Well . . .
(*He starts for the door.*)

BILL

(*Takes* HERB's *arm and they go into the hall*)
I'm going over to the Dean's for supper, Herb. If you're through with Tom come by here and I'll walk you part way to the station.

HERB

All right. (*Stops on the stairs*) How do you talk to the boys, Bill?

BILL

I don't know. I just talk to them.

HERB

They're not your sons. I only talked with Tom, I mean, really talked with him, once before. It was after a Sunday dinner and I made up my mind it was time we sat in a room together and talked about important things. He got sick to his stomach. That's a terrible effect to have on your boy . . . Well, I'll drop down.

64

(*He takes a roll of money from his pocket and looks at it, then starts up the stairs.*)

BILL

(*Coming into his study*)

Laura, you shouldn't try to tell him about his own son. After all, if he doesn't know the boy, who does?

LAURA

I'm sorry.

(BILL *exits into the other part of the house, pulling off his tie.* HERB *has gone up the stairs. Knocks on the study door.* LAURA *settles down in her chair and eventually goes on with her sewing.*)

AL

(*Inside, calls*)

Come in.

(HERB *goes in and shuts the door.*)

HERB

(*Opens* TOM's *bedroom door and sticks his head in*)

Hello, there.

TOM

(*Looks up from the bed, surprised*)

Oh . . . Hi . . .

HERB

I got held up at the Dean's.

TOM

Oh.

(*He has risen, and attempts to kiss his father on the cheek. But his father holds him off with a firm handshake.*)

HERB

How's everything? You look bushed.

TOM

I'm okay.

HERB

(*Looking at him closely*)

You sure?

TOM

Sure.

HERB

(*Looking around room*)

This room looks smaller than I remember. (*He throws on light switch*) I used to have the bed over here. Used to rain in some nights. (*Comes across phonograph*) This the one I gave you for Christmas?

TOM

Yeah. It works fine.

HERB

(*Turns phonograph off*)

You're neater than I was. My vest was always behind the radiator, or somewhere. (*Sees part of dress costume*) What's this?

TOM

(*Hesitates for a moment. Then*)

A costume Mrs. Reynolds made for me. I'm in the play.

HERB

You didn't write about it.

TOM

I know.

HERB

What are you playing?

(*Looks at dress.*)

TOM

You know *The School For Scandal*. I'm playing Lady Teazle.

HERB

Tom, I want to talk to you. Last time we tried to talk, it didn't work out so well.

TOM

What's up?

HERB

Tom, I'd like to be your friend. I guess there's something between fathers and sons that keeps them from being friends, but I'd like to try.

TOM

(*Embarrassed*)

Sure, Dad.
> (*He sits on the bed.*)

HERB

Now when you came here, I told you to make friends slowly. I told you to make sure they were the right kind of friends. You're known by the company you keep. Remember I said that?

TOM

Yes.

HERB

And I told you if you didn't want to go out for sports like football, hockey . . . that was all right with me. But you'd get in with the right kind of fellow if you managed these teams. They're usually pretty good guys. You remember.

TOM

Yes.

HERB

Didn't you believe me?

68

TOM

Yes, I believed you.

HERB

Okay, then let's say you believed me, but you decided to go your own way. That's all right too, only you see what it's led to.

TOM

What?

HERB

You made friends with people like this Harris guy who got himself fired.

TOM

Why is he getting fired?

HERB

He's being fired because he was seen in the dunes with you.

TOM

Look, I don't—

HERB

Naked.

TOM

You too?

69

HERB

So you know what I'm talking about?

TOM

No, I don't.

HERB

You do too know. I heard my sister tell you once. She warned you about a janitor in the building down the street.

TOM

(*Incredulous*)

Mr. Harris . . . ?

HERB

Yes. He's being fired because he's been doing a lot of suspicious things around apparently, and this finished it. All right, I'll say it plain, Tom. He's a fairy. A homosexual.

TOM

Who says so?

HERB

Now, Tom—

TOM

And seeing us on the beach . . .

HERB

Yes.

70

TOM

And what does that make me?

HERB

Listen, I know you're all right.

TOM

Thanks.

HERB

Now wait a minute.

TOM

Look, we were just swimming.

HERB

All right, all right. So perhaps you didn't know.

TOM

What do you mean perhaps?

HERB

It's the school's fault for having a guy like that around. But it's your fault for being a damned fool in picking your friends.

TOM

So that's what the guys meant.

HERB

You're going to get a ribbing for a while, but you're going to be a man about it and you're going to take it and you're going to come through much more careful how you make your friends.

TOM

He's kicked out because he was seen with me on the beach, and I'm telling you that nothing, absolutely nothing . . . Look, I'm going to the Dean and tell him that Harris did nothing, that—

HERB

(*Stopping him*)
Look, don't be a fool. It's going to be hard enough for you without sticking your neck out, asking for it.

TOM

But, Dad!

HERB

He's not going to be reappointed next year. Nothing you can say is going to change anyone's mind. You got to think about yourself. Now, first of all, get your hair cut. (TOM *looks at father, disgusted*) Look, this isn't easy for me. Stop thinking about yourself, and give me a break. (TOM *looks up at this appeal*) I suppose you think it's going to be fun for *me* to have to live this down back home. It'll get around, and it'll affect me, too. So we've got to see this thing through together. You've got to do your part. Get your hair cut. And then . . . No, the first thing I want you to do is call whoever is putting on this play, and tell them you're not playing this lady whatever her name is.

TOM

Why shouldn't I play it? It's the best part in the play, and I was chosen to play it.

HERB

I should think you'd have the sense to see why you shouldn't.

TOM

Wait a minute. You mean . . . do you mean, you think I'm . . . whatever you call it? Do you, Dad?

HERB

I told you "no."

TOM

But the fellows are going to think that I'm . . . and Mrs. Reynolds?

HERB

Yes. You're going to have to fight their thinking it. Yes.
(TOM *sits on the bed, the full realization of it dawning.*)

RALPH

(*Sticks his head around the stairs from upstairs,
and yells*)
Hey, Grace, who's taking you to the dance Saturday night? Hey, Grace!
(*He disappears again up the stairs.*)

73

HERB

What's that all about?

TOM

I don't know.
(LAURA, *as the noise comes in, rises and goes to door to stop it, but* AL *comes into the hall and goes upstairs yelling at the boys and* LAURA *goes back to her chair.*)

HERB

(*Looks at his watch*)
Now . . . Do you want me to stay over? If I'm not going to stay over tonight, I've got to catch the six-fifty-four.

TOM

Stay over?

HERB

Yes, I didn't bring a change of clothes along, but if you want me to stay over . . .

TOM

Why should you stay over?

HERB

(*Stung a little by this*)
All right. Now come on down to Bill's room and telephone this drama fellow. So I'll know you're making a start of it. And bring the dress.

TOM

I'll do it tomorrow.

74

HERB

I'd feel better if you did it tonight. Come on. I'm walking out with Bill. And incidentally, the Dean said if the ribbing goes beyond bounds . . . you know . . . you're to come to him and he'll take some steps. He's not going to do anything now, because these things take care of themselves. They're better ignored . . .

(*They have both started out of the bedroom, but during the above* HERB *goes back for the dress.* TOM *continues out and stands on the stairs looking at the telephone in the hall.*)

HERB

(*Comes out of the study. Calls back*)

See you Al. Take good care of my boy here. (*Starts down stairs. Stops*) You need any money?

TOM

No.

HERB

I'm lining you up with a counselor's job at camp this year. If this thing doesn't spoil it. (*Stops*) You sure you've got enough money to come home?

TOM

Yes, sure. Look Dad, let me call about the play from here. (*He takes receiver off hook.*)

HERB

Why not use Bill's phone? He won't mind. Come on. (TOM *reluctantly puts phone back on hook*) Look, if you've got any

75

problems, talk them over with Bill—Mr. Reynolds. He's an old friend, and I think he'd tell you about what I'd tell you in a spot. (*Goes into master's study*) Is Bill ready?

LAURA

He'll be right down. How does the costume work?

TOM

I guess it's all right, only . . .

HERB

I'd like Tom to use your phone if he may—to call whoever's putting on the play. He's giving up the part.

LAURA

Giving up the part?

HERB

Yes. I've . . . I want him to. He's doing it for me.

LAURA

Mr. Lee, it was a great honor for him to be chosen to play the part.

HERB

Bill will understand. Bill! (*He thrusts costume into* LAURA's *hand and goes off through alcove*) Bill, what's the number of the man putting on the play. Tom wants to call him.

(LAURA *looks at* TOM *who keeps his eyes from her. She makes a move towards him, but he takes a step away.*)

BILL

(*Off stage*)

Fred Mayberry . . . Three–two–six . . . You ready, Herb?

HERB

(*Off stage*)

Yes. You don't mind if Tom uses your phone, do you?

BILL

Of course not.

HERB

(*Comes in*)

When do you go on your mountain-climbing week-end, Bill?

BILL

(*Comes in*)

This week-end's the outing.

HERB

Maybe Tom could go with you.

BILL

He's on the dance committee, I think. Of course he's welcome if he wants to. Always has been.

HERB

(*Holding out phone to* TOM)

Tom. (TOM *hesitates to cross to phone. As* LAURA *watches*

77

him with concern, he makes a move to escape out the door)
Three–two–six.

> (TOM *slowly and painfully crosses the stage, takes the*
> *phone and sits.)*

BILL

Will you walk along with us as far as the dining hall,
Laura?

LAURA

I don't think I feel like supper, thanks.

BILL

> (*Looks from her to* TOM)

What?

HERB

I've got to get along if I want to catch my train.
> (TOM *dials phone.*)

BILL

Laura?
> (LAURA *shakes her head, tight-lipped.*)

HERB

Well, then, good-bye, Laura . . . I still like you.

LAURA

Still going to the Dean's, Bill?

BILL

Yes. I'll be right back after supper. Sure you don't want to walk along with us to the dining hall?
(LAURA *shakes her head.*)

TOM

Busy.

HERB
(Pats his son's arm)
Keep trying him. We're in this together. Anything you want? (TOM *shakes his head "no"*) Just remember, anything you want, let me know. (*To* LAURA) See you at reunion time . . . This'll all be blown over by then.
(He goes.)

BILL

Laura, I wish you'd . . . Laura!
(He is disturbed by her mood. He sees it's hopeless, and goes after HERB, *leaving door open.*)*

TOM
(At phone)
Hello, Mr. Mayberry . . . This is Tom Lee . . . Yes, I know it's time to go to supper, Mr. Mayberry . . . (*Looks around at open door.* LAURA *shuts it*) but I wanted you to know . . . (*This comes hard*) I wanted you to know I'm not going to be able to play in the play . . . No . . . I . . . well, I just can't.
(He is about to break. He doesn't trust himself to speak.)

79

LAURA

(*Quickly crosses and takes phone from* TOM)
Give it to me. Hello, Fred . . . Laura. Yes, Tom's father, well, he wants Tom—he thinks Tom is tired, needs to concentrate on his final exams. You had someone covering the part, didn't you? . . . Yes, of course it's a terrible disappointment to Tom. I'll see you tomorrow.

(*She hangs up.* TOM *is ashamed and humiliated. Here is the woman he loves, hearing all about him . . . perhaps believing the things . . .* LAURA *stands above him for a moment, looking at the back of his head with pity. Then he rises and starts for the door without looking at her.* RALPH *and* STEVE *come stampeding down the stairway.*)

RALPH

(*As he goes*)
Okay, you can sit next to him if you want. Not me.

STEVE

Well, if you won't . . . why should I?

RALPH

Two bits nobody will.

(*They slam out the front door.* TOM *has shut the door quickly again when he has heard* RALPH *and* STEVE *start down. Now stands against the door listening.*)

AL

(*Comes out from his door, pulling on his jacket. Calls*)
Tom . . . Tom!

(*Getting no answer, he goes down the stairs and out.*)

LAURA

Tom . . .

TOM

(*Opens the study door*)

I'll bet my father thinks I'm . . .

(*Stops.*)

LAURA

Now, Tom! I thought I'd call Joan Harrison and ask her to come over for tea tomorrow. I want you to come too. I want you to ask her to go to the dance with you.

TOM

(*Turns in anguish and looks at her for several moments. Then*)

You were to go with me.

LAURA

I know, but . . .

TOM

Do you think so too, like the others? Like my father?

LAURA

Tom!

TOM

Is that why you're shoving me off on Joan?

LAURA

(*Moving towards him*)

Tom, I asked her over so that we could lick this thing.

81

TOM

(Turns on her)

What thing? What thing?

(He looks at her a moment, filled with indignation, then he bolts up the stairs. But on the way up, PHIL is coming down. TOM feels like a trapped rat. He starts to turn down the stairs again, but he doesn't want to face LAURA, as he is about to break. He tries to hide his face and cowers along one side going up.)

PHIL

What's the matter with you?

(TOM doesn't answer. Goes on up and into the study door. PHIL shrugs his shoulders and goes on down the stairs and out. TOM comes into his own bedroom and shuts the door and leans against the doorjamb. LAURA goes to the partly opened door. Her impulse is to go up to TOM to comfort him, but she checks herself, and turns in the doorway and closes the door, then walks back to her chair and sits down and reaches out and touches the teapot, as though she were half-unconsciously rubbing out a spot. She is puzzled and worried. Upstairs we hear the first few sobs from TOM as the lights dim out, and

THE CURTAIN FALLS

ACT TWO

ACT TWO

Scene I

The scene is the same.
The time is two days later.
As the curtain rises, AL *is standing at the public telephone fastened to the wall on the first landing. He seems to be doing more listening than talking.*

AL

Yeah . . . (*He patiently waits through a long tirade*) Yeah, Dad. I know, Dad . . . No, I haven't done anything about it, yet . . . Yes, Mr. Hudson says he has a room in his house for me next year . . . But I haven't done anything about it here yet . . . Yeah, okay, Dad . . . I know what you mean . . . (*Gets angry*) I swear to God I don't . . . I lived with him a year, and I don't . . . All right, okay, Dad . . . No, don't *you* call. I'll do it. Right now.

> (*He hangs up. He stands and puts his hands in his pocket and tries to think this out. It's something he doesn't like.*)

RALPH

(*Comes in the house door and starts up the steps*)
Hey, Al?

AL

Yeah?

RALPH

The guys over at the Beta house want to know has it happened yet?

AL

Has what happened?

RALPH

Has Tom made a pass at you yet?

AL

(*Reaches out to swat* RALPH)
For crying out loud!

RALPH

Okay, okay! You can borrow my chastity belt if you need it.

AL

That's not funny.

RALPH

(*Shifting his meaning to hurt* AL)
No, I know it's not. The guys on the ball team don't think it's funny at all.

AL

What do you mean?

RALPH

The guy they're supposed to elect captain rooming with a queer.

AL

(*Looks at him for a moment, then rejects the idea*)
Aw ... knock it off, huh!

RALPH

So you don't believe me ... Wait and see. (*Putting on a dirty grin*) Anyway, my mother said I should save myself for the girl I marry. Hell, how would you like to have to tell your wife, "Honey, I've been saving myself for you, except for one night when a guy—" (AL *roughs* RALPH *up with no intention of hurting him*) Okay, okay. So you don't want to be captain of the baseball team. So who the hell cares. I don't, I'm sure.

AL

Look. Why don't you mind your own business?

RALPH

What the hell fun would there be in that?

AL

Ralph, Tom's a nice kid.

RALPH

Yeah. That's why all the guys leave the shower room at the gym when he walks in.

AL

When?

RALPH

Yesterday ... Today. You didn't hear about it?

AL

No. What are they trying to do?

RALPH

Hell, they don't want some queer looking at them and—

AL

Oh, can it! Go on up and bury your horny nose in your *Art Models* magazine.

RALPH

At least I'm normal. I like to look at pictures of naked girls, not men, the way Tom does.

AL

Jeeze, I'm gonna push your face in in a—

RALPH

Didn't you notice all those strong man poses he's got in his bottom drawer?

AL

Yes, I've noticed them. His old man wants him to be a muscle man, and he wrote away for this course in muscle building and they send those pictures. Any objections?

RALPH

Go on, stick up for him. Stick your neck out. You'll get it chopped off with a baseball bat, you crazy bastard.

(*Exits upstairs.* AL *looks at the phone, then up the way* RALPH *went. He is upset. He throws himself into a few*

88

push-ups, using the bannisters. Then still not happy with what he's doing, he walks down the stairs and knocks on the study door.)

LAURA

(Comes from inside the house and opens the door)
Oh, hello, Al.

AL

Is Mr. Reynolds in?

LAURA

Why, no, he isn't. Can I do something?

AL

I guess I better drop down when he's in.

LAURA

All right. I don't really expect him home till after supper tonight.

AL

(Thinks for a moment)
Well . . . well, you might tell him just so's he'll know and can make other plans . . . I won't be rooming in this house next year. This is the last day for changing, and I want him to know that.

LAURA

(Moves into the room to get a cigarette)
I see. Well, I know he'll be sorry to hear that, Al.

89

AL

I'm going across the street to Harmon House.

LAURA

Both you and Tom going over?

AL

No.

LAURA

Oh.

AL

Just me.

LAURA

I see. Does Tom know this?

AL

No. I haven't told him.

LAURA

You'll have to tell him, won't you, so he'll be able to make other plans.

AL

Yes, I suppose so.

LAURA

Al, won't you sit down for a moment, please? (AL *hesitates, but comes in and sits down. Offers* AL *a cigarette*) Cigarette?

AL

(*Reaches for one automatically, then stops*)
No, thanks. I'm in training.

(*He slips a pack of cigarettes from his shirt pocket to his trousers pocket.*)

LAURA

That's right. I'm going to watch you play Saturday afternoon. (AL *smiles at her*) You're not looking forward to telling Tom, are you, Al? (AL *shakes his head, "No"*) I suppose I can guess why you're not rooming with him next year. (AL *shrugs his shoulders*) I wonder if you know how much it has meant for him to room with you this year. It's done a lot for him too. It's given him a confidence to know he was rooming with one of the big men of the school.

AL

(*Embarrassed*)
Oh . . .

LAURA

You wouldn't understand what it means to be befriended. You're one of the strong people. I'm surprised, Al.

AL

(*Blurting it out*)
My father's called me three times. How he ever found out about Harris and Tom, I don't know. But he did. And some guy called him and asked him, "Isn't that the boy your son is rooming with?" . . . and he wants me to change for next year.

LAURA

What did you tell your father?

AL

I told him Tom wasn't so bad, and . . . I'd better wait and see Mr. Reynolds.

LAURA

Al, you've lived with Tom. You know him better than anyone else knows him. If you do this, it's as good as finishing him so far as this school is concerned, and maybe farther.

AL

(*Almost whispering it*)
Well, he *does* act sort of queer, Mrs. Reynolds. He . . .

LAURA

You never said this before. You never paid any attention before. What do you mean, "queer?"

AL

Well, like the fellows say, he sort of walks lightly, if you know what I mean. Sometimes the way he moves . . . the things he talks about . . . long hair music all the time.

LAURA

All right. He wants to be a singer. So he talks about it.

AL

He's never had a girl up for any of the dances.

92

LAURA

Al, there are good explanations for all these things you're saying. They're silly . . . and prejudiced . . . and arguments all dug up to suit a point of view. They're all after the fact.

AL

I'd better speak to Mr. Reynolds.
(*He starts for the door.*)

LAURA

Al, look at me.
(*She holds his eyes for a long time, wondering whether to say what she wants to say.*)

AL

Yes?

LAURA

(*She decides to do it*)
Al, what if I were to start the rumor tomorrow that you were . . . well, queer, as you put it.

AL

No one would believe it.

LAURA

Why not?

AL

Well, because . . .

LAURA

Because you're big and brawny and an athlete. What they call a top guy and a hard hitter?

93

AL

Well, yes.

LAURA

You've got some things to learn, Al. I've been around a little, and I've met men, just like you—same setup—who weren't men, some of them married and with children.

AL

Mrs. Reynolds, you wouldn't do a thing like that.

LAURA

No, Al, I probably wouldn't. But I could, and I almost would to show you how easy it is to smear a person, and once I got them believing it, you'd be surprised how quickly your . . . manly virtues would be changed into suspicious characteristics.

AL

(*Has been standing with his hands on his hips.* LAURA *looks pointedly at this stance.* AL *thrusts his hands down to his side, and then behind his back*)

Mrs. Reynolds, I got a chance to be captain of the baseball team next year.

LAURA

I know. And I have no right to ask you to give up that chance. But I wish somehow or other you could figure out a way . . . so it wouldn't hurt Tom.

(TOM *comes in the hall and goes up the stairs. He's pretty broken up, and mad. After a few moments he appears in his room, shuts the door, and sits on the bed, trying to figure something out.*)

AL
(As TOM *enters house)*

Well . . .

LAURA

That's Tom now. (AL *looks at her, wondering how she knows*) I know all your footsteps. He's coming in for tea. (AL *starts to move to door*) Well, Al? (AL *makes a helpless motion*) You still want me to tell Mr. Reynolds about your moving next year?

AL
(After a moment)

No.

LAURA

Good.

AL

I mean, I'll tell him when I see him.

LAURA

Oh.

AL
(Turns on her)

What can I do?

LAURA

I don't know.

AL

Excuse me for saying so, but it's easy for you to talk the way you have. You're not involved. You're just a bystander. You're not going to be hurt. Nothing's going to happen to you one way or the other. I'm sorry.

LAURA

That's a fair criticism, Al. I'm sorry I asked you . . . As you say, I'm not involved.

AL

I'm sorry. I think you're swell, Mrs. Reynolds. You're the nicest housemaster's wife I've ever ran into . . . I mean . . . Well, you know what I mean. It's only that . . . (*He is flustered. He opens the door*) I'm sorry.

LAURA

I'm sorry, too, Al.
> (*She smiles at him.* AL *stands in the doorway for a moment, not knowing whether to go out the hall door or go upstairs. Finally, he goes upstairs, and into the study door.* LAURA *stands thinking over what* AL *has said, even repeating to herself, "I'm not involved." She then goes into the alcove and off.*)

AL

> (*Outside* TOM's *bedroom door*)

Tom? (TOM *moves quietly away from the door*) Tom? (*He opens the door*) Hey.

TOM

I was sleeping.

AL

Standing up, huh? (TOM *turns away*) You want to be alone?

TOM

No. You want to look. Go ahead.
(*He indicates the window.*)

AL

No, I don't want to look, I ... (*He looks at* TOM, *not knowing how to begin ... He stalls ... smiling*) Nice tie you got there.

TOM

(*Starts to undo tie*)
Yeah, it's yours. You want it?

AL

No. Why? I can only wear one tie at a time. (TOM *leaves it hanging around his neck. After an awkward pause*) I ... uh ...

TOM

I guess I don't need to ask you what's the matter?

AL

It's been rough today, huh?

TOM

Yeah. (*He turns away, very upset. He's been holding it in ... but here's his closest friend asking him to open up*) Jesus

97

Christl! (AL *doesn't know what to say. He goes to* TOM's *bureau and picks up his hairbrush, gives his hair a few brushes*) Anybody talk to you?

AL

Sure. You know they would.

TOM

What do they say?

AL

(*Yanks his tie off*)
Hell, I don't know.

TOM

I went to a meeting of the dance committee. I'm no longer on the dance committee. Said that since I'd backed out of playing the part in the play, I didn't show the proper spirit. That's what they *said* was the reason.

AL

(*Loud*)
Why the hell don't you do something about it?

TOM

(*Yelling back*)
About what?

AL

About what they're saying.

TOM

What the hell can I do?

AL

Geez, you could . . . (*He suddenly wonders what* TOM *could do*) I don't know.

TOM

I tried to pass it off. Christ, you can't pass it off. You know, when I went into the showers today after my tennis match, everyone who was in there, grabbed a towel and . . . and . . . walked out.

AL

They're stupid. Just a bunch of stupid bastards.
(*He leaves the room.*)

TOM

(*Following him into sitting room*)
Goddamn it, the awful thing I found myself . . . Jesus, I don't know . . . I found myself self-conscious about things I've been doing for years. Dressing, undressing . . . I keep my eyes on the floor . . . (*Re-enters his own room*) Geez, if I even look at a guy that doesn't have any clothes on, I'm afraid someone's gonna say something, or . . . Jesus, I don't know.

AL

(*During this,* AL *has come back into the room, unbuttoning his shirt, taking it off, etc. Suddenly he stops*)
What the hell am I doing? I've had a shower today.
(*He tries to laugh.*)

99

TOM

(*Looks at him a moment*)

Undress in your own room, will ya? You don't want them talking about you too, do you?

AL

No I don't.

(*He has said this very definitely and with meaning.*)

TOM

(*Looks up at his tone of voice*)

Of course you don't. (*He looks at* AL *a long time. He hardly dares say this*) You . . . uh . . . you moving out?

AL

(*Doesn't want to answer*)

Look, Tom, do you mind if I try to help you?

TOM

Hell, no. How?

AL

I know this is gonna burn your tail, and I know it sounds stupid as hell. But it isn't stupid. It's the way people look at things. You could do a lot for yourself, just the way you talk and look.

TOM

You mean get my hair cut?

AL

For one thing.

TOM

Why the hell should a man with a crew cut look more manly than a guy who—

AL

Look, I don't know the reasons for these things. It's just the way they are.

TOM

(*Looking at himself in bureau mirror*)
I tried a crew cut a coupla times. I haven't got that kind of hair, or that kind of head. (*After a moment*) Sorry, I didn't mean to yell at you. Thanks for trying to help.

AL

(*Finds a baseball on the radiator and throws it at* TOM. TOM *smiles, and throws it back*)
Look, Tom, the way you walk . . .

TOM

Oh, Jesus.

AL

(*Flaring*)
Look, I'm trying to help you.

TOM

No one gave a goddamn about how I walked till last Saturday!

101

AL
(Starts to go)

Okay, okay. Forget it.
(He goes out.)

TOM
(Stands there a few moments, then slams the baseball into the bed and walks out after AL *into sitting room)*

Al?

AL
(Off)

Yeah?

TOM

Tell me about how I walk.

AL
(In the sitting room)

Go ahead, walk!

TOM
(Walks back into the bedroom. AL *follows him, wiping his face on a towel and watching* TOM *walk. After he has walked a bit)*

Now I'm not going to be able to walk any more. Everything I been doing all my life makes me look like a fairy.

AL

Go on.

TOM

All right, now I'm walking. Tell me.

AL

Tom, I don't know. You walk sort of light.

TOM

Light?
(*He looks at himself take a step.*)

AL

Yeah.

TOM

Show me.

AL

No, I can't do it.

TOM

Okay. You walk. Let me watch you. I never noticed how you walked. (AL *stands there for a moment, never having realized before how difficult it could be to walk if you think about it. Finally he walks*) Do it again.

AL

If you go telling any of the guys about this . . .

TOM

Do you think I would? . . . (AL *walks again*) That's a good walk. I'll try to copy it. (*He tries to copy the walk, but never*

103

succeeds in taking even a step) Do you really think that'll make any difference?

AL

I dunno.

TOM

Not now it won't. Thanks anyway.

AL

(Comes and sits on bed beside TOM. *Puts his arm around* TOM's *shoulder and thinks this thing out)*
Look, Tom . . . You've been in on a lot of bull sessions. You heard the guys talking about stopping over in Boston on the way home . . . getting girls . . . you know.

TOM

Sure. What about it?

AL

You're not going to the dance Saturday night?

TOM

No. Not now.

AL

You know Ellie Martin. The gal who waits on table down at the soda joint?

TOM

Yeah. What about her?

AL

You've heard the guys talking about her.

TOM

Come on, come on.

AL

Why don't you drop in on Ellie Saturday night?

TOM

What do you mean?

AL

Hell, do you want me to draw a picture?

TOM
(*With disgust*)

Ellie Martin?

AL

Okay. I know she's a dog, but . . .

TOM

So what good's that going to do? I get caught there, I get thrown out of school.

AL

No one ever gets caught. Sunday morning people'd hear about it . . . not the Dean . . . I mean the fellows. Hell, Ellie tells and tells and tells . . . Boy, you'd be made!

TOM

Are you kidding?

AL

No.

TOM

(*With disgust*)

Ellie Martin!

AL

(*After a long pause*)

Look, I've said so much already, I might as well be a complete bastard . . . You ever been with a woman?

TOM

What do you think?

AL

I don't think you have.

TOM

So?

AL

You want to know something?

TOM

What?

AL

Neither have I. But if you tell the guys, I'll murder you.

TOM

All those stories you told . . .

AL

Okay, I'll be sorry I told you.

TOM

Then why don't you go see Ellie Martin Saturday night?

AL

Why the hell should I?

TOM

You mean you don't have to prove anything?

AL

Aw, forget it. It's probably a lousy idea anyway.
(*He starts out.*)

TOM

Yeah.

AL

(*Stops*)

Look, about next—
(*Stops.*)

TOM

Next year? Yes?

AL

Hap Hudson's asked me to come to his house. He's got a

single there. A lot of the fellows from the team are over there, and ... well ...

(*He doesn't look at* TOM.)

TOM

Sure, sure ... I understand.

AL

Sorry I didn't tell you till now, after we'd made our plans. But I didn't know. I mean, I just found out about the ... the opening.

TOM

I understand!

AL

(*Looks up at last. He hates himself but he's done it, and it's a load off his chest*)

See ya.

(*He starts to go.*)

TOM

(*As* AL *gets to door*)

Al ... (AL *stops and looks back. Taking tie from around his neck*) Here.

AL

(*Looks at tie, embarrassed*)

I said wear it. Keep it.

TOM

It's yours.

108

AL

(*Looks at the tie for a long time, then without taking it, goes through the door*)

See ya.

> (TOM *folds the tie neatly, dazed, then seeing what he's doing, he throws it viciously in the direction of the bureau, and turns and stares out the window. He puts a record on the phonograph.*)

BILL

(*Comes in to the study from the hall, carrying a pair of shoes and a slim book. As he opens his study door, he hears the music upstairs. He stands in the door and listens, remembering his miserable boyhood. Then he comes in and closes the door*)

Laura.

> (*Throws shoes on floor near footstool.*)

LAURA

(*Off stage, calling*)

Bill?

BILL

Yes.

LAURA

(*Coming in with tea things*)

I didn't think you'd be back before your class. Have some tea.

BILL

I beat young Harvey at handball.

LAURA

Good.

BILL

At last. It took some doing, though. He was after my scalp because of that D minus I gave him in his last exam. (*Gives her book*) You wanted this . . . book of poems.

LAURA

(*Looks at book. Her eyes shift quickly to the same book in the chair*)

Why yes. How did you know?

BILL

(*Trying to be very offhand about it*)

The notice from the bookstore.

LAURA

That's very nice of you.

(*She moves towards him to kiss him, but at this moment, in picking some wrapping paper from the armchair, he notices the duplicate copy.*)

BILL

(*A little angry*)

You've already got it.

LAURA

Why, yes . . . I . . . well, I . . . (BILL *picking it up . . . opens it*) That is, someone gave it to me. (BILL *reads the inscription*) Tom knew I wanted it, and . . .

BILL

(*Looks at her, a terrible look coming into his face. Then he slowly rips the book in two and hurls it into the fireplace*) Damn!

LAURA

Bill! (BILL *goes to footstool and sits down and begins to change his shoes*) Bill, what difference does it make that he gave me the book? He knew I wanted it too.

BILL

I don't know. It's just that every time I try to do something . . .

LAURA

Bill, how can you say that? It isn't so.

BILL

It is.

LAURA

Bill, this thing of the book is funny.

BILL

I don't think it's very funny.

LAURA

(*Going behind him, and kneeling by his side*) Bill, I'm very touched that you should have remembered. Thank you. (*He turns away from her and goes on with his shoes*) Bill, don't turn away. I want to thank you. (*As she gets no response from him, she rises*) Is it such a chore to let yourself be thanked? (*She puts her hands on his shoulders, trying*

111

to embrace him) Oh, Bill, we so rarely touch any more. I keep feeling I'm losing contact with you. Don't you feel that?

BILL

(*Looking at his watch*)

Laura, I . . .

LAURA

(*She backs away from him*)

I know, you've got to go. But it's just that, I don't know, we don't touch any more. It's a silly way of putting it, but you seem to hold yourself aloof from me. A tension seems to grow between us . . . and then when we do . . . touch . . . it's a violent thing . . . almost a compulsive thing. (BILL *is uncomfortable at this accurate description of their relationship. He sits troubled. She puts her arms around his neck and embraces him, bending over him*) You don't feel it? You don't feel yourself holding away from me until it becomes overpowering? There's no growing together any more . . . no quiet times, just holding hands, the feeling of closeness, like it was in Italy. Now it's long separations and then this almost brutal coming together, and . . . Oh, Bill, you do see, you do see. (BILL *suddenly straightens up, toughens, and looks at her.* LAURA *repulsed, slowly draws her arms from around his shoulders.*)

BILL

For God's sake, Laura, what are you talking about? (*He rises and goes to his desk*) It can't always be a honeymoon. (*Upstairs in his room,* TOM *turns off the phonograph, and leaves the room, going out into the hall and up the stairs.*)

LAURA

Do you think that's what I'm talking about?

BILL

I don't know why you chose a time like this to talk about things like . . .

LAURA

. . . I don't know why, either. I just wanted to thank you for the book . . . (*Moves away and looks in book*) What did you write in it?

BILL

(*Starts to mark exam papers*)
Nothing. Why? Should I write in it? I just thought you wanted the book.

LAURA

Of course . . . Are you sure you won't have some tea?
(*She bends over the tea things.*)

BILL

Yes.

LAURA

(*Straightening up, trying another tack of returning to normality*)
Little Joan Harrison is coming over for tea.

BILL

No, she isn't. (LAURA *looks inquiringly*) I just saw her father

at the gym. I don't think that was a very smart thing for you
to do, Laura.

LAURA

I thought Tom might take her to the dance Saturday. He's
on the committee, and he has no girl to take.

BILL

I understand he's no longer on the committee. You're a
hostess, aren't you?

LAURA

Yes.

BILL

I've got the mountain-climbing business this week-end.
Weather man predicts rain.

LAURA

(*Almost breaks. Hides her face in her hands. Then recovers*)
That's too bad. (*After a moment*) Bill?

BILL

Yes?

LAURA

I think someone should go to the Dean about Tom and
the hazing he's getting.

BILL

What could the Dean do? Announce from chapel, "You've
got to stop riding Tom. You've got to stop calling him Grace?"
Is that what you'd like him to do?

LAURA

No. I suppose not.

BILL

You know we're losing Al next year because of Tom.

LAURA

Oh, you've heard?

BILL

Yes, Hudson tells me he's moving over to his house. He'll probably be captain of the baseball team. Last time we had a major sport captain was eight years ago.

LAURA

Yes, I'm sorry.

BILL

However, we'll also be losing Tom.

LAURA

Oh?

BILL

(*Noting her increased interest*)

Yes. We have no singles in this house, and he'll be rooming alone.

LAURA

I'm sorry to hear that.

BILL

(*He turns to look at her*)

I knew you would be.

LAURA

Why should my interest in this boy make you angry?

BILL

I'm not angry.

LAURA

You're not only angry. It's almost as though you were, well, jealous.

BILL

Oh, come on now.

LAURA

Well, how else can you explain your . . . your vindictive attitude towards him?

BILL

Why go into it again? Jealous! (*He has his books together now. Goes to the door*) I'll go directly from class to the dining hall. All right?

LAURA

Yes, of course.

BILL

And please, please, Laura . . .
  (*He stops.*)

LAURA

I'll try.

BILL

I know you like to be different, just for the sake of being different . . . and I like you for that . . . But this time, lay off. Show your fine free spirit on something else.

LAURA

On something that can't hurt us?

BILL

All right. Sure. I don't mind putting it that way. And Laura?

LAURA

Yes?

BILL

Seeing Tom so much . . . having him down for tea alone all the time . . .

LAURA

Yes?

BILL

I think you should have him down only when you have the other boys . . . for his own good. I mean that. Well, I'll see you in the dining hall. Try to be on time. (*He goes out.* LAURA *brings her hands to her face, and cries, leaning against the back of the chair.* AL *has come tumbling out of the door to his room with books in hand, and is coming down the stairs. Going down the hall*) You going to class, Al?

117

AL

Hello, Mr. Reynolds. Yes I am.

BILL

(*As they go*)
Let's walk along together. I'm sorry to hear that you're moving across the street next year.
(*And they are gone out the door.*)

TOM

(*Has come down the stairs, and now stands looking at the hall telephone. He is carrying his coat. After a long moment's deliberation, he puts in a coin and dials*)
Hello, I'd like to speak to Ellie Martin, please. (LAURA *has moved to pick up the torn book which her husband has thrown in the fireplace. She is smoothing it out, as she suddenly hears* TOM's *voice in the hall. She can't help but hear what he is saying. She stands stock still and listens, her alarm and concern showing on her face*) Hello, Ellie? This is Tom Lee . . . Tom Lee. I'm down at the soda fountain all the time with my roommate, Al Thompson . . . Yeah, the guys do sometimes call me that . . . Well, I'll tell you what I wanted. I wondered if . . . you see, I'm not going to the dance Saturday night, and I wondered if you're doing anything? Yeah, I guess that is a hell of a way to ask for a date . . . but I just wondered if I could maybe drop by and pick you up after work on Saturday . . . I don't know what's *in* it for you, Ellie . . . but something I guess. I just thought I'd like to see you . . . What time do you get through work? . . . Okay, nine o'clock. (LAURA, *having heard this, goes out through the alcove. About to hang up*) Oh, thanks.

(*He stands for a moment, contemplating what he's done, then he slips on his jacket, and goes to the study door and knocks. After a moment, he opens the door and enters.*)

LAURA

(*Coming from the other room with a plate of cookies*)
Oh, there you are. I've got your favorites today.

TOM

Mrs. Reynolds, do you mind if I don't come to tea this afternoon?

LAURA

Why . . . if you don't want to . . . How are you?
(*She really means this question.*)

TOM

I'm okay.

LAURA

Good.

TOM

It's just I don't feel like tea.

LAURA

Perhaps, it's just as well . . . Joan can't make it today, either.

TOM

I didn't expect she would. She's nothing special; just a kid.

119

LAURA

Something about a dentist appointment or something.

TOM

It wouldn't have done any good anyway. I'm not going to the dance.

LAURA

Oh?

TOM

Another member of the committee will stop around for you.

LAURA

What will you be doing?

TOM

I don't know. I can take care of myself.

LAURA

If you're not going, that gives me an easy out. I won't have to go.

TOM

Just because I'm not going?

LAURA

(*In an effort to keep him from going to Ellie*)
Look, Tom . . . now that neither of us is going, why don't you drop down here after supper, Saturday night. We could listen to some records, or play gin, or we can just talk.

TOM

I . . . I don't think you'd better count on me.

LAURA

I'd like to.

TOM

No, really. I don't want to sound rude . . . but I . . . I may
have another engagement.

LAURA

Oh?

TOM

I'd like to come. Please understand that. It's what I'd like
to do . . . but . . .

LAURA

Well, I'll be here just in case, just in case you decide to
come in. (LAURA *extends her hand*) I hope you'll be feeling
better.

TOM

(*Hesitates, then takes her hand*)
Thanks.

LAURA

Maybe your plans will change.
(TOM *looks at her, wishing they would; knowing they
won't. He runs out and down the hall as the lights fade
out on* LAURA *standing at the door.*)

CURTAIN

SCENE II

The time is eight-forty-five on Saturday night.

In the study a low fire is burning. As the curtain rises, the town clock is striking the three quarter hour. LAURA *is sitting in her chair sipping a cup of coffee. The door to the study is open slightly. She is waiting for* TOM. *She is wearing a lovely but informal dress, and a single flower. In his room,* TOM *listens to the clock strike. He has just been shaving. He is putting shaving lotion on his face. His face is tense and nervous. There is no joy in the preparations. In a moment, he turns and leaves the room, taking off his belt as he goes.*

After a moment, LILLY *comes to the study door, knocks and comes in.*

LILLY

Laura?

LAURA

Oh, Lilly.

LILLY

(Standing in the doorway, a raincoat held over her head. She is dressed in a low-cut evening gown, which she wears very well)

You're not dressed yet. Why aren't you dressed for the dance?

LAURA

(*Still in her chair*)
I'm not going. I thought I told you.

LILLY

(*Deposits raincoat and goes immediately to look at herself in mirror next to the door*)
Oh, for Heaven's sake, why not? Just because Bill's away with his loathesome little mountain climbers?

LAURA

Well . . .

LILLY

Come along with us. It's raining on and off, so Harry's going to drive us in the car.

LAURA

No, thanks.

LILLY

If you come, Harry will dance with you all evening. You won't be lonely, I promise you. (LAURA *shakes her head, "no"*) You're the only one who can dance those funny steps with him.

LAURA

It's very sweet of you, but no.

LILLY

(*At the mirror*)
Do you think this neck is too low?

LAURA

I think you look lovely.

LILLY

Harry says this neck will drive all the little boys crazy.

LAURA

I don't think so.

LILLY

Well, that's not very flattering.

LAURA

I mean, I think they'll appreciate it, but as for driving them crazy . . .

LILLY

After all I want to give them some reward for dancing their duty dances with me.

LAURA

I'm sure when they dance with you, it's no duty, Lilly. I've seen you at these dances.

LILLY

It's not this . . . (*Indicating her bosom*) it's my line of chatter. I'm oh so interested in what courses they're taking, where they come from and where they learned to dance so divinely.

LAURA

(*Laughing*)

Lilly, you're lost in a boys' school. You were meant to shine some place much more glamorous.

LILLY

I wouldn't trade it for the world. Where else could a girl indulge in three hundred innocent flirtations a year?

LAURA

Lilly, I've often wondered what you'd do if one of the three hundred attempted to go, well, a little further than innocent flirtation.

LILLY

I'd slap him down . . . the little beast. (*She laughs and admires herself in mirror*) Harry says if I'm not careful I'll get to looking like Ellie Martin. You've seen Ellie.

LAURA

I saw her this afternoon for the first time.

LILLY

Really? The first time?

LAURA

Yes. I went into the place where she works . . . the soda shop . . .

LILLY

You!

LAURA

Yes . . . uh . . . for a package of cigarettes. (*After a moment she says with some sadness*) She's not even pretty, is she?

LILLY

(*Turns from admiring herself at the tone in* LAURA's *voice*)
Well, honey, don't sound so sad. What difference should it make to you if she's pretty or not?

LAURA

I don't know. It just seems so . . . they're so young.

LILLY

If they're stupid enough to go to Ellie Martin, they deserve whatever happens to them. Anyway, Laura, the boys *talk* more about Ellie than anything else. So don't fret about it.

LAURA

(*Arranges chair for* TOM *facing fireplace. Notices* LILLY *primping*)
You look lovely, Lilly.

LILLY

Maybe I'd better wear that corsage the dance committee sent, after all . . . right here. (*She indicates low point in dress*) I was going to carry it—or rather Harry was going to help me carry it. You know, it's like one of those things people put on Civil War monuments on Decoration Day.

LAURA

Yes, I've seen them.

LILLY

(*Indicating the flower* LAURA *is wearing*)
Now that's tasteful. Where'd you get that?

LAURA

Uh . . . I bought it for myself.

LILLY

Oh, now.

LAURA

It's always been a favorite of mine and I saw it in the florist's window.

LILLY

Well, Harry will be waiting for me to tie his bow tie. (*Starts towards door*) Will you be up when we get back?

LAURA

(*Giving* LILLY *her raincoat*)
Probably not.

LILLY

If there's a light on, I'll drop in and tell you how many I had to slap down . . . Night-night.
(*She leaves.* LAURA *stands at the closed door until she hears the outside door close. Then she opens her door a bit. She takes her cup of coffee and stands in front of the fireplace and listens.*)

TOM

(*As* LILLY *goes, he returns to his room, dressed in a blue suit. He stands there deliberating a moment, then reaches*

127

*under his pillow and brings out a pint bottle of whisky. He
takes a short swig. It gags him. He corks it and puts it back
under the pillow)*

Christ, I'll never make it.

> *(He reaches in his closet and pulls out a raincoat, then
> turns and snaps out the room light, and goes out. A
> moment later, he appears on the stairs. He sees
> LAURA's door partly open, and while he is putting on
> his raincoat, he walks warily past it.)*

LAURA

*(When she hears TOM's door close, she stands still and listens
more intently. She hears him pass her door and go to the front
door. She puts down the cup of coffee, and goes to the study
door. She calls)*

Tom? *(After some moments, TOM appears in the door, and
she opens it wide)* I've been expecting you.

TOM

I . . . I . . .

LAURA

(Opening the door wide)
Are you going to the dance, after all?

TOM

(Comes in the door)
No . . . You can report me if you want. Out after hours.
Or . . . *(He looks up at her finally)* Or you can give me permission. Can I have permission to go out?

TEA AND SYMPATHY

LAURA

(*Moving into the room, says pleasantly*)
I think I'd better get you some coffee.

TOM

(*At her back, truculent*)
You can tell them that, too . . . that I've been drinking.
There'll be lots to tell before—(*He stops*) I didn't drink much.
But I didn't eat much either.

LAURA

Let me get you something to eat.

TOM

(*As though convincing himself*)
No. I can't stay!

LAURA

All right. But I'm glad you dropped in. I was counting on
it.

TOM

(*Chip on shoulder*)
I said I might not. When you invited me.

LAURA

I know. (*She looks at him a moment. He is to her a heartbreaking sight . . . all dressed up as though he were going to
a prom, but instead he's going to Ellie . . . the innocence and
the desperation touch her deeply . . . and this shows in her
face as she circles behind him to the door*) It's a nasty night
out, isn't it?

TOM

Yes.

LAURA

I'm just as glad I'm not going to the dance. (*She shuts the door gently.* TOM, *at the sound of the door, turns and sees what she has done*) It'll be nice just to stay here by the fire.

TOM

I wasn't planning to come in.

LAURA

Then why the flower . . . and the card? "For a pleasant evening?"

TOM

It was for the dance. I forgot to cancel it.

LAURA

I'm glad you didn't.

TOM

Why?
 (*He stops studying the curtains and looks at her.*)

LAURA

(*Moving into the room again*)
Well, for one thing I like to get flowers. For another thing . . . (TOM *shakes his head a little to clear it*) Let me make you some coffee.

TOM

No. I'm just about right.

LAURA

Or you can drink this . . . I just had a sip. (*She holds up the cup.* TOM *looks at the proferred coffee*) You can drink from this side.
(*She indicates the other side of the cup.*)

TOM

(*Takes the cup, and looks at the side where her lips have touched and then slowly turns it around to the other and takes a sip*)
And for another thing?

LAURA

What do you mean?

TOM

For one thing you like to get flowers . . .

LAURA

For another it's nice to have flowers on my anniversary.

TOM

Anniversary?

LAURA

Yes.

131

TOM

(*Waving the cup and saucer around*)
And Mr. Reynolds on a mountain top with twenty stalwart youths, soaking wet . . . Didn't he remember?

LAURA

(*Rescues the cup and saucer*)
It's not that anniversary. (TOM *looks at her wondering. Seeing that she has interested him, she moves towards him*) Let me take your coat.

TOM

(*Definitely*)
I can't—

LAURA

I know. You can't stay. But . . . (*She comes up behind him and puts her hand on his shoulders to take off his coat. He can hardly stand her touch. She gently peels his coat from him and stands back to look at him*) How nice you look!

TOM

(*Disarranging his hair or tie*)
Put me in a blue suit and I look like a kid.

LAURA

How did you know I liked this flower?

TOM

You mentioned it.

LAURA

You're very quick to notice these things. So was he.

TOM

(After a moment, his curiosity aroused)
Who?

LAURA

My first husband. That's the anniversary.

TOM

I didn't know.

LAURA

(Sits in her chair)
Mr. Reynolds doesn't like me to talk about my first husband. He was, I'd say, about your age. How old are you, Tom?

TOM

Eighteen . . . tomorrow.

LAURA

Tomorrow . . . We must celebrate.

TOM

You'd better not make any plans.

LAURA

He was *just* your age then. *(She looks at him again with slight wonder)* It doesn't seem possible now, looking at you . . .

133

TOM

Why, do I look like such a child?

LAURA

Why no.

TOM

Men are married at my age.

LAURA

Of course, they are. *He* was. Maybe a few months older. Such a lonely boy, away from home for the first time . . . and . . . and going off to war. (TOM *looks up inquiringly*) Yes, he was killed.

TOM

I'm sorry . . . but I'm glad to hear about him.

LAURA

Glad?

TOM

Yes. I don't know . . . He sounds like someone you *should* have been married to, not . . . (*Stops*) I'm sorry if I . . .
(*Stops.*)

LAURA

(*After a moment*)
He was killed being conspicuously brave. He had to be conspicuously brave, you see, because something had hap-

pened in training camp . . . I don't know what . . . and he
was afraid the others thought him a coward . . . He showed
them he wasn't.

TOM

He had that satisfaction.

LAURA

What was it worth if it killed him?

TOM

I don't know. But I can understand.

LAURA

Of course you can. You're very like him.

TOM

Me?

LAURA

(*Holding out the coffee cup*)
Before I finish it all? (TOM *comes over and takes a sip from
his side of the cup*) He was kind and gentle, and lonely. (TOM
turns away in embarrassment at hearing himself so described)
We knew it wouldn't last . . . We sensed it . . . But he always
said, "Why must the test of everything be its durability?"

TOM

I'm sorry he was killed.

LAURA

Yes, so am I. I'm sorry he was killed the way he was killed
. . . trying to prove how brave he was. In trying to prove he
was a man, he died a boy.

TOM

Still he must have died happy.

LAURA

Because he proved his courage?

TOM

That . . . and because he was married to you. (*Embarrassed, he walks to his coat which she has been holding in her
lap*) I've got to go.

LAURA

Tom, please.

TOM

I've got to.

LAURA

It must be a very important engagement.

TOM

It is.

LAURA

If you go now, I'll think I bored you, talking all about myself.

TOM

You haven't.

LAURA

I probably shouldn't have gone on like that. It's just that I felt like it . . . a rainy spring night . . . a fire. I guess I'm in a reminiscent mood. Do you ever get in reminiscing moods on nights like this?

TOM

About what?

LAURA

Oh, come now . . . there must be something pleasant to remember, or someone. (TOM *stands by the door beginning to think back, his raincoat in his hand, but still dragging on the floor*) Isn't there? . . . Of course there is. Who was it, or don't you want to tell?

TOM

(*After a long silence*)
May I have a cigarette?

LAURA

(*Relieved that she has won another moment's delay*)
Yes. Of course.
(*Hands him a box, then lights his cigarette.*)

TOM

My seventh-grade teacher.

LAURA

What?

TOM

That's who I remember.

LAURA

Oh.

TOM

Miss Middleton . . .

LAURA

How sweet.

TOM

(*Drops the raincoat again, and moves into the room*)
It wasn't sweet. It was terrible.

LAURA

At that time, of course . . . Tell me about her.

TOM

She was just out of college . . . tall, blonde, honey-colored
hair . . . and she wore a polo coat, and drove a convertible.

LAURA

Sounds very fetching.

TOM

Ever since then I've been a sucker for girls in polo coats.

LAURA

(*Smiling*)

I have one somewhere.

TOM

Yes, I know.
(*He looks at her.*)

LAURA

What happened?

TOM

What could happen? As usual I made a fool of myself. I guess everyone knew I was in love with her. People I like, I can't help showing it.

LAURA

That's a good trait.

TOM

When she used to go on errands and she needed one of the boys to go along and help carry something, there I was.

LAURA

She liked you too, then.

TOM

This is a stupid thing to talk about.

LAURA

I can see why she liked you.

TOM

I thought she . . . I thought she loved me. I was twelve years old.

LAURA

Maybe she did.

TOM

Anyway, when I was in eighth grade, she got married. And you know what they made me do? They gave a luncheon at school in her honor, and I had to be the toastmaster and wish her happiness and everything . . . I had to write a poem . . . (*He quotes*)

"Now that you are going to be married,
And away from us be carried,
Before you promise to love, honor and obey,
There are a few things I want to say."

(*He shakes his head as they both laugh*) From there on it turned out to be more of a love poem than anything else.

LAURA

(*As she stops laughing*)
Puppy love can be heartbreaking.

TOM

(*The smile dying quickly as he looks at her. Then after what seems like forever*)
I'm always falling in love with the wrong people.

TEA AND SYMPATHY

LAURA

Who isn't?

TOM

You too?

LAURA

It wouldn't be any fun if we didn't. Of course, nothing ever comes of it, but there are bittersweet memories, and they can be pleasant. (*Kidding him as friend to friend, trying to get him to smile again*) Who else have you been desperately in love with?

TOM

(*He doesn't answer. Then he looks at his watch*)
It's almost nine . . . I'm late.
(*Starts to go.*)

LAURA

(*Rising*)
I can't persuade you to stay? (TOM *shakes his head, "no"*)
We were getting on so well.

TOM

Thanks.

LAURA

In another moment I would have told you all the deep, dark secrets of my life.

TOM

I'm sorry.
(*He picks up his coat from the floor.*)

LAURA

(*Desperately trying to think of something to keep him from going*)

Won't you stay even for a dance?

TOM

I don't dance.

LAURA

I was going to teach you.
(*She goes over to the phonograph and snaps on the button.*)

TOM

(*Opens the door*)

Some other time . . .

LAURA

Please, for me.
(*She comes back.*)

TOM

(*After a moment he closes the door*)

Tell me something.

LAURA

Yes?
(*The record starts to play, something soft and melodic. It plays through to the end of the act.*)

TOM

Why are you so nice to me?

LAURA

Why . . . I . . .

TOM

You're not this way to the rest of the fellows.

LAURA

No, I know I'm not. Do you mind my being nice to you?

TOM

(*Shakes his head, "no"*)
I just wondered why.

LAURA

(*In a perfectly open way*)
I guess, Tom . . . I guess it's because I like you.

TOM

No one else seems to. Why do you?

LAURA

I don't know . . . I . . .

TOM

Is it *because* no one else likes me? Is it just pity?

LAURA

No, Tom, no, of course not . . . It's, well . . . it's because you've been very nice to me . . . very considerate. It wasn't

easy for me, you know, coming into a school, my first year.
You seemed to sense that. I don't know, we just seem to have
hit it off.

(*She smiles at him.*)

TOM

Mr. Reynolds knows you like me.

LAURA

I suppose so. I haven't kept it a secret.

TOM

Is that why he hates me so?

LAURA

I don't think he hates you.

TOM

Yes, he hates me. Why lie? I think everyone here hates me
but you. But they won't.

LAURA

Of course they won't.

TOM

He hates me because he made a flop with me. I know all
about it. My father put me in this house when I first came
here, and when he left me he said to your husband, "Make
a man out of him." He's failed, and he's mad, and then you
came along, and were nice to me . . . out of pity.

144

LAURA

No, Tom, not pity. I'm too selfish a woman to like you just out of pity.

TOM

(*He has worked himself up into a state of confusion, and anger, and desperation*)
There's so much I . . . there's so much I don't understand.

LAURA

(*Reaches out and touches his arm*)
Tom, don't go out tonight.

TOM

I've got to. That's one thing that's clear. I've got to!

LAURA

(*Holds up her arms for dancing*)
Won't you let me teach you how to dance?

TOM

(*Suddenly and impulsively he throws his arms around her, and kisses her passionately, awkwardly, and then in embarrassment he buries his head in her shoulder*)
Oh, God . . . God.

LAURA

Tom . . . Tom . . . (TOM *raises his face and looks at her, and would kiss her again*) No, Tom . . . No, I . . . (*At the first "No,"* TOM *breaks from her and runs out the door halfway up the stairs. Calling*) Tom! . . . Tom! (TOM *stops at the sound of her voice and turns around and looks down the stairs.* LAURA *moves to the open door*) Tom, I . . . (*The front door opens and two of the mountain-climbing boys,* PHIL *and* PAUL *come in, with their packs.*)

PHIL

(*Seeing* TOM *poised on the stairs*)
What the hell are you doing? (TOM *just looks at him*) What's the matter with you?

(*He goes on and up the stairs.*)

TOM

What are you doing back?

PAUL

The whole bunch is back. Who wants to go mountain climbing in the rain?

BILL

(*Outside his study door*)
Say, any of you fellows want to go across the street for something to eat when you get changed, go ahead. (PHIL *and* PAUL *go up the stairs past* TOM. BILL *goes into his own room, leaving door open*) Hi. (*He takes off his equipment and puts it on the floor.*)

LAURA

(*Has been standing motionless where* TOM *has left her*)
Hello.

BILL

(*Comes to her and kisses her on the cheek*)
One lousy week-end a year we get to go climbing and it rains. (*Throws the rest of his stuff down*) The fellows are damned disappointed.

LAURA

(*Hardly paying any attention to him*)
That's too bad.

BILL

(*Going up to alcove*)
I think they wanted me to invite them down for a feed. But I didn't want to. I thought we'd be alone. Okay?
(*He looks across at her.*)

LAURA

(*She is listening for footsteps outside*)
Sure. (BILL *goes out through alcove.* LAURA *stoops and picks up the raincoat which* TOM *has dropped and hides it in the cabinet by the fireplace.*)

BILL

(*Appears in door momentarily wiping his hands with towel*)
Boy it really rained. (*He disappears again.* LAURA *sadly goes to the door and slowly and gently closes it. When she is finished, she leans against the door, listening, hoping against hope that* TOM *will go upstairs. When* TOM *sees the door close, he stands there for a moment, then turns his coat collar up and goes down the hall and out. Off stage as* TOM

147

starts to go down the hall) We never made it to the timber-line. The rain started to come down. Another hour or so and we would have got to the hut and spent the night, but the fellows wouldn't hear of it . . . (*The door slams.* LAURA *turns away from the study door in despair. Still off stage*) What was that?

LAURA

Nothing . . . Nothing at all.

BILL

(*Enters and gets pipe from mantelpiece*)
Good to get out, though. Makes you feel alive. Think I'll go out again next Saturday, alone. Won't be bothered by the fellows wanting to turn back.

(*He has settled down in the chair intended for* TOM. *The school bells start to ring nine.* BILL *reaches out his hand for* LAURA. *Standing by the door, she looks at his outstretched hand, as the lights fade, and*

THE CURTAIN FALLS

ACT THREE

ACT THREE

The time is late the next afternoon.

As the curtain rises, TOM is in his room. His door is shut and bolted. He is lying on his back on the bed, staring up at the ceiling.

RALPH

(He is at the phone)

Hello, Mary . . . Ralph . . . Yeah, I just wanted you to know I'd be a little delayed picking you up . . . Yeah . . . everyone was taking a shower over here, and there's only one shower for eight guys . . . No it's not the same place as last night . . . The tea dance is at the Inn . . . (*He suddenly looks very uncomfortable*) Look, I'll tell you when I see you . . . Okay . . . (*Almost whispers it*) I love you . . . (STEVE, RALPH's *sidekick, comes running in from the outside. He's all dressed up and he's got something to tell*) Yeah, Mary. Well, I can't say it over again . . . Didn't you hear me the first time? (*Loud so she'll hear it*) Hi, Steve.

STEVE

Come on, get off. I got something to tell you.

RALPH

Mary—Mary, I'll get there faster if I stop talking now. Okay? Okay. See you a little after four. (*He hangs up*) What the hell's the matter with you?

STEVE

Have you seen Tom?

RALPH

No.

STEVE

You know what the hell he did last night?

RALPH

What?

STEVE

He went and saw Ellie.

RALPH

Who are you bulling?

STEVE

No, honest. Ellie told Jackson over at the kitchen. Everybody knows now.

RALPH

What did he want to go and do a thing like that for?

STEVE

But wait a minute. You haven't heard the half of it.

RALPH

Listen, I gotta get dressed.
(*Starts upstairs.*)

STEVE

(*On their way up the stairs*)
The way Ellie tells it, he went there, all the hell dressed
up like he was going to the dance, and . . .

(*They disappear up the stairs.* BILL *after a moment,
comes in the hall, and goes quickly up the stairs. He
goes right into* AL *and* TOM's *main room without knocking. We then hear him try the handle of* TOM's *bedroom door.* TOM *looks at the door defiantly and sul-
lenly.*)

BILL

(*Knocks sharply*)
Tom! (*Rattles door some more*) Tom, this is Mr. Reynolds.
Let me in.

TOM

I don't want to see anyone.

BILL

You've got to see me. Come on. Open up! I've got to talk
to the Dean at four, and I want to speak to you first.

TOM

There's nothing to say.

BILL

I can break the door down. Then your father would have
to pay for a new door. Do you want that? Are you afraid
to see me? (TOM *after a moment, goes to the door and pulls*

back the bolt. BILL *comes in quickly*) Well. (TOM *goes back and sits on the bed. Doesn't look at* BILL) Now I've got to have the full story. All the details so that when I see the Dean . . .

TOM

You've got the full story. What the hell do you want?

BILL

We don't seem to have the full story.

TOM

When the school cops brought me in last night they told you I was with Ellie Martin.

BILL

That's just it. It seems you weren't *with* her.

TOM

(*After a moment*)
What do you mean?

BILL

You weren't *with* her. You couldn't be *with* her. Do you understand what I mean?

TOM

(*Trying to brave it out*)
Who says so?

BILL

She says so. And she ought to know. (TOM *turns away*) She says that you couldn't . . . and that you jumped up and grabbed a knife in her kitchen and tried to kill yourself . . . and she had to fight with you and that's what attracted the school cops.

TOM

What difference does it make?

BILL

I just wanted the record to be straight. You'll undoubtedly be expelled, no matter what . . . but I wanted the record straight.

TOM

(*Turning on him*)
You couldn't have stood it, could you, if I'd proved you wrong?

BILL

Where do you get off talking like that to a master?

TOM

You'd made up your mind long ago, and it would have killed you if I'd proved you wrong.

BILL

Talking like that isn't going to help you any.

TOM

Nothing's going to help. I'm gonna be kicked out, and then you're gonna be happy.

BILL

I'm not going to be happy. I'm going to be very sorry . . . sorry for your father.

TOM

All right, now you know. Go on, spread the news. How can you wait?

BILL

I won't tell anyone . . . but the Dean, of course.

TOM

And my father . . .

BILL

Perhaps . . .

TOM

(*After a long pause*)
And Mrs. Reynolds.

BILL

(*Looks at* TOM)
Yes. I think she ought to know. (*He turns and leaves the room. Goes through the sitting room and up the stairs, calling "Ralph."* TOM *closes the door and locks it, goes and sits down in the chair.*)

LAURA

(*As* BILL *goes upstairs to* RALPH, *she comes into the master's study. She is wearing a wool suit. She goes to the cupboard and brings out* TOM's *raincoat. She moves with it to the door. There is a knock. She opens the door*)
Oh, hello, Mr. Lee.

HERB

(*Coming in, he seems for some reason rather pleased*)
Hello, Laura.

LAURA

Bill isn't in just now, though I'm expecting him any moment.

HERB

My train was twenty minutes late. I was afraid I'd missed him. We have an appointment with the Dean in a few minutes . . .

LAURA

(*Is coolly polite*)
Oh, I see.

HERB

Have I done something to displease you, Laura? You seem a little . . .
(HERB *shrugs and makes a gesture with his hands meaning cool.*)

LAURA

I'm sorry. Forgive me. Won't you sit down?

HERB

I remember that you were displeased at my leaving Tom in school a week ago. Well, you see I was right in a sense. Though, perhaps being a lady you wouldn't understand.

LAURA

I'm not sure that I do.

HERB

Well, now, look here. If I had taken Tom out of school after that scandal with Mr. . . . . uh . . . what was his name?

LAURA

Mr. Harris.

HERB

Yes. If I'd taken Tom out then, he would have been marked for the rest of his life.

LAURA

You know that Tom will be expelled, of course.

HERB

Yes, but the circumstances are so much more normal.

LAURA

(*After looking at him a moment*)
I think, Mr. Lee, I'm not quite sure, but I think, in a sense, you're proud of Tom.

158

HERB

Well.

LAURA

Probably for the first time you're proud of him because the school police found him out of bounds with a . . .

HERB

I shouldn't have expected you to understand. Bill will see what I mean.

(BILL *starts down the stairs.*)

LAURA

Yes. He probably will.

(BILL *comes in the room.*)

HERB

Bill.

BILL

Hello, Herb.

(HERB *looks from* LAURA *to* BILL. *Notices the coldness between them.*)

BILL

I was just up seeing Tom.

HERB

Yes. I intend to go up after we've seen the Dean. How is he?

BILL

All right.

HERB

(*Expansive*)
Sitting around telling the boys all about it.

BILL

No, he's in his room alone. The others are going to the tea dance at the Inn. Laura . . . (*Sees* LAURA *is leaving the room*) Oh, Laura, I wish you'd stay.

(LAURA *takes one step back into the room.*)

HERB

I was telling your wife here, trying to make her understand the male point of view on this matter. I mean, how being kicked out for a thing like this, while not exactly desirable, is still not so serious. It's sort of one of the calculated risks of being a man.

(*He smiles at his way of putting it.*)

BILL

(*Preparing to tell* HERB)
Herb?

HERB

Yes, Bill. I mean, you agree with me on that, don't you?

BILL

Yes, Herb, only the situation is not exactly as it was reported to you over the phone. It's true that Tom went to this girl Ellie's place, and it's true that he went for the usual purpose. However . . . however, it didn't work out that way.

HERB

What do you mean?

BILL

Nothing happened.

HERB

You mean she . . . she wouldn't have him?

BILL

I mean, Tom . . . I don't know . . . he didn't go through with it. He couldn't. (*He looks at* LAURA) It's true. The girl says so. And when it didn't work, he tried to kill himself with a knife in the kitchen, and she struggled with him, and that brought the school cops, and that's that. (LAURA *turns away, shocked and moved.* MR. LEE *sits down in a chair bewildered*) I'm sorry, Herb. Of course the fact that he was with Ellie at her place is enough to get him expelled.

HERB

Does everyone know this?

BILL

Well, Ellie talks. She's got no shame . . . and this is apparently something to talk about.

LAURA

(*To* MR. LEE)
Do you still think it will make a good smoking-car story?

BILL

What do you mean?

HERB

Why did he do it? Before, maybe he could talk it down, but to go do a thing like this and leave no doubts.

LAURA

In whose mind?

BILL

Laura, please.

LAURA
(*Angry*)
You asked me to stay.

BILL
(*Flaring back at her*)
Well, now you've heard. We won't keep you.

LAURA
(*Knowing, without asking*)
Why did you want me to hear?

BILL
(*Going to her*)
I wanted you to know the facts. That's all. The whole story.
(LAURA *stands in the alcove.*)

162

HERB

Bill, Bill! Maybe there's some way of getting to this girl so she wouldn't spread the story.

BILL

I'm afraid it's too late for that.

HERB

I don't know. Some things don't make any sense. What am I going to do now?

LAURA
(*Re-entering*)
Mr. Lee, please don't go on drawing the wrong conclusions!

HERB

I'm drawing no conclusions. This sort of thing can happen to a normal boy. But it's what the others will think . . . Added to the Harris business. And that's all that's important. What they'll think.

LAURA

Isn't it important what Tom thinks?

BILL

Herb, we'd better be getting on over to the Dean's . . .

HERB
(*Indicating upstairs*)
Is he in his room?

163

BILL

Yes.

HERB

Packing?

BILL

No.

HERB

I told him to come to you to talk things over. Did he?

BILL

No.

HERB

What am I going to say to him now?

BILL

We're expected at four.

HERB

I know. But I've got to go up . . . Maybe I should have left him with his mother. She might have known what to do, what to say . . . (*He starts out*) You want to come along with me?

BILL

(*Moving to hall*)

All right.

LAURA

(*Serious*)

Bill, I'd like to talk with you.

BILL

I'll be back.

(*Goes with* HERB *to the landing.* LAURA *exits, taking off her jacket.*)

HERB

Maybe I ought to do this alone.

BILL

He's probably locked in his bedroom.

(HERB *goes up the stairs and inside the study.* BILL *stays in the hall.* TOM, *as he hears his father knocking on the bedroom door, stiffens.* HERB *tries the door handle.*)

HERB

(*Off, in the study*)

Tom . . . Tom . . . it's Dad. (TOM *gets up, but just stands there*) Tom, are you asleep? (*After a few moments, he reappears on the landing. He is deeply hurt that his son wouldn't speak to him*) I think he's asleep.

BILL

(*Making a move to go in and get* TOM)

He can't be . . .

165

HERB

(*Stops*)

Yes, I think he is. He was always a sound sleeper. We used to have to drag him out of bed when he was a kid.

BILL

But he should see you.

HERB

It'll be better later, anyhow.
(*He starts down the stairs, troubled, puzzled.*)

BILL

I'll go right with you, Herb.
(*They re-enter the study, and* BILL *goes out through the alcove.* HERB *stays in the master's study.*)

TOM

(*When his father is downstairs, he opens his bedroom door and faintly calls*)

Dad?
(HERB *looks up, thinking he's heard something but then figures it must have been something else.* RALPH, STEVE *and* PHIL *come crashing down the stairs, dressed for the tea dance, ad libbing comments about the girls at the dance.* TOM *closes his door. When they have gone, he opens it again and calls "Dad" faintly. When there is no response, he closes the door, and goes and lies on the bed.*)

BILL

(Re-entering)

Laura, I'm going to the Dean's now with Herb. I'm playing squash with the headmaster at five. So I'll see you at the
dining room at six-thirty.

LAURA

(Entering after him)

I wish you'd come back here after.

BILL

Laura, I can't.

LAURA

Bill, I wish you would.

BILL

(Sees that there is some strange determination in LAURA'S
face)

Herb, I'll be with you in a minute. Why don't you walk
along?

HERB

All right . . . Good-bye, Laura. See you again.

BILL

You'll see her in a couple of days at the reunion.

HERB

I may not be coming up for it now . . . Maybe I will. I

don't know. I'll be walking along. Good-bye, Laura. Tell
Tom I tried to see him.

(*He goes out.*)

BILL

Now, Laura, what's the matter? I've got to get to the
Dean's rooms to discuss this matter.

LAURA

Yes, of course. But first I'd like to discuss the boys who
made him do this . . . the men and boys who made him do
this.

BILL

No one made him do anything.

LAURA

Is there to be no blame, no punishment for the boys and
men who taunted him into doing this? What if he had succeeded in killing himself? What then?

BILL

You're being entirely too emotional about this.

LAURA

If he had succeeded in killing himself in Ellie's rooms,
wouldn't you have felt some guilt?

BILL

I?

LAURA

Yes, you.

168

BILL

I wish you'd look at the facts and not be so emotional about this.

LAURA

The facts! What facts! An innocent boy goes swimming with an instructor . . . an instructor whom he likes because this instructor is one of the few who encourage him, who don't ride him . . . And because he's an off-horse, you and the rest of them are only too glad to put two and two together and get a false answer . . . anything which will let you go on and persecute a boy whom you basically don't like. If it had happened with Al or anybody else, you would have done nothing.

BILL

It would have been an entirely different matter. You can't escape from what you are . . . your character. Why do they spend so much time in the law courts on character witnesses? To prove this was the kind of man who could or couldn't commit such and such a crime.

LAURA

I resent this judgment by prejudice. He's not like me, therefore, he is capable of all possible crimes. He's not one of us . . . a member of the tribe!

BILL

Now look, Laura, I know this is a shock to you, because you were fond of this boy. But you did all you could for him, more than anyone would expect. After all, your responsibility doesn't go beyond—

169

LAURA

I know. Doesn't go beyond giving him tea and sympathy on Sunday afternoons. Well, I want to tell you something. It's going to shock you . . . but I'm going to tell you.

BILL

Laura, it's late.

LAURA

Last night I knew what Tom had in mind to do.

BILL

How did you know?

LAURA

I heard him making the date with Ellie on the phone.

BILL

And you didn't stop him? Then you're the one responsible.

LAURA

Yes, I am responsible, but not as you think. I did try to stop him, but not by locking him in his room, or calling the school police. I tried to stop him by being nice to him, by being affectionate. By showing him that he was liked . . . yes, even loved. I knew what he was going to do . . . and why he was going to do it. He had to prove to you bullies that he was a man, and he was going to prove it with Ellie Martin. Well . . . last night . . . last night, I wished he had proved it with me.

BILL

What in Christ's name are you saying?

LAURA

Yes, I shock you. I shock myself. But you are right. I am responsible here. I know what I should have done. I knew it then. My heart cried out for this boy in his misery . . . a misery imposed by my husband. And I wanted to help him as one human being to another . . . and I failed. At the last moment, I sent him away . . . sent him to . . .

BILL

You mean you managed to overcome your exaggerated sense of pity.

LAURA

No, it was not just pity. My heart in its own loneliness . . . Yes, I've been lonely here, miserably lonely . . . and my heart in its loneliness cried out for this boy . . . cried out for the comfort he could give me too.

BILL

You don't know what you're saying.

LAURA

But I was a good woman. Good in what sense of the word? Good to whom . . . and for whom?

BILL

Laura, we'll discuss this, if we must, later on . . .

171

LAURA

Bill! There'll be no later on. I'm leaving you.

BILL

Over this thing?

LAURA

(*After a moment*)
Yes, this *thing*, and all the other *things* in our marriage.

BILL

For God's sake, Laura, what are you talking about?

LAURA

I'm talking about love and honor and manliness, and tenderness, and persecution. I'm talking about a lot. You haven't understood any of it.

BILL

Laura, you can't leave over a thing like this. You know what it means.

LAURA

I wouldn't worry too much about it. When I'm gone, it will probably be agreed by all that I was an off-horse too, and didn't really belong to the clan, and it's good riddance.

BILL

And you're doing this . . . all because of this . . . this fairy?

LAURA

(After a moment)
This boy, Bill . . . this boy is more of a man than you are.

BILL

Sure. Ask Ellie.

LAURA

Because it was distasteful for him. Because for him there has to be love. He's more of a man than you are.

BILL

Yes, sure.

LAURA

Manliness is not all swagger and swearing and mountain climbing. Manliness is also tenderness, gentleness, consideration. You men think you can decide on who is a man, when only a woman can really know.

BILL

Ellie's a woman. Ask Ellie.

LAURA

I don't need to ask anyone.

BILL

What do you know about a man? Married first to that boy . . . again, a poor pitiable boy . . . You want to mother a boy, not love a man. That's why you never really loved me. Because I was not a boy you could mother.

LAURA

You're quite wrong about my not loving you. I did love you. But not just for your outward show of manliness, but because you needed me . . . For one unguarded moment you let me know you needed me, and I have tried to find that moment again the year we've been married . . . Why did you marry me, Bill? In God's name, why?

BILL

Because I loved you. Why else?

LAURA

You've resented me . . . almost from the day you married me, you've resented me. You never wanted to marry really . . . Did they kid you into it? Does a would-be headmaster have to be married? Or what was it, Bill? You would have been far happier going off on your jaunts with the boys, having them to your rooms for feeds and bull sessions . . .

BILL

That's part of being a master.

LAURA

Other masters and their wives do not take two boys always with them whenever they go away on vacations or weekends.

BILL

They are boys without privileges.

LAURA

And I became a wife without privileges.

174

BILL

You became a wife . . .
(*He stops.*)

LAURA

Yes?

BILL

You did *not* become a wife.

LAURA

I know. I know I failed you. In some terrible way I've failed you.

BILL

You were more interested in mothering that fairy up there than in being my wife.

LAURA

But you wouldn't let me, Bill. You wouldn't let me.

BILL

(*Grabbing her by the shoulders*)
What do you mean I wouldn't let you?

LAURA

(*Quietly, almost afraid to say it*)
Did it ever occur to you that you persecute in Tom, that boy up there, you persecute in him the thing you fear in yourself? (BILL *looks at her for a long moment of hatred. She has hit close to the truth he has never let himself be conscious of. There is a moment when he might hurt her, but then he*

175

draws away, still staring at her. He backs away, slowly, and then turns to the door) Bill!

BILL

(Not looking at her)

I hope you will be gone when I come back from dinner.

LAURA

(Quietly)

I will be . . . (*Going towards him*) Oh, Bill, I'm sorry. I shouldn't have said that . . . it was cruel. (*She reaches for him as he goes out the door*) This was the weakness you cried out for me to save you from, wasn't it . . . And I have tried. (*He is gone*) I have tried. (*Slowly she turns back into the room and looks at it*) I did try. (*For a few minutes she stands stunned and tired from her outburst. Then she moves slowly to* TOM's *raincoat, picks it up and turns and goes out of the room and to the stair-landing. She goes to the boy's study door and knocks*) Tom. (*She opens it and goes in out of sight. At* TOM's *door, she calls again)* Tom. (TOM *turns his head slightly and listens.* LAURA *opens* TOM's *door and comes in*) Oh, I'm sorry. May I come in? (*She sees she's not going to get an answer from him, so she goes in*) I brought back your raincoat. You left it last night. (*She puts it on chair. She looks at him*) This is a nice room . . . I've never seen it before . . . As a matter of fact I've never been up here in this part of the house. (*Still getting no response, she goes on.* TOM *slowly turns and looks at her back, while she is examining something on the walls. She turns, speaking*) It's very cozy. It's really quite . . . (*She stops when she sees he has turned around looking at her*) Hello.

that's what just
happened last night
problem: (as if tried 2
last make, attack etc
night own mother.

TEA AND SYMPATHY

TOM
(*Barely audible*)

Hello.

LAURA

Do you mind my being here?

TOM

You're not supposed to be.

LAURA

I know. But everyone's out, and will be for some time . . .
I wanted to return your raincoat.

TOM

Thank you. (*After a pause he sits up on the bed, his back to her*) I didn't think you'd ever want to see me again.

LAURA

Why not?

TOM

After last night. I'm sorry about what happened downstairs.

LAURA
(*She looks at him a while, then*)

I'm not.

TOM
(*Looks at her. Can't quite make it out*)

You've heard everything, I suppose.

TOM- boy who has met with the most
serious problem of his life + the
outcome has already been decided by
those who don't understand him.
accused of crime did not commit.

LAURA

Yes.

TOM

Everything?

LAURA

Everything.

TOM

I knew your husband would be anxious to give you the details.

LAURA

He did.

(*She stands there quietly looking down at the boy.*)

TOM

So now you know too.

LAURA

What?

TOM

That everything they said about me is true.

LAURA

Tom!

TOM

Well, it is, isn't it?

LAURA

Tom?

TOM

I'm no man. Ellie knows it. Everybody knows it. It seems everybody knew it, except me. And now I know it.

LAURA

(Moves towards him)

Tom . . . Tom . . . dear. (TOM *turns away from her*) You don't think that just because . . .

TOM

What else am I to think?

LAURA

(Very gently)

Tom, that didn't work because you didn't believe in it . . . in such a test.

TOM

(With the greatest difficulty)

I touched her, and there was nothing.

LAURA

You aren't in love with Ellie.

TOM

That's not supposed to matter.

LAURA

But it does.

179

Ellie - diseased

TOM

I wish they'd let me kill myself.

LAURA

Tom, look at me. (TOM *shakes his head*) Tom, last night you kissed me.

TOM

Jesus!

LAURA

Why did you kiss me?

TOM

(*Turns suddenly*)
And it made you sick, didn't it? Didn't it?
(*Turns away from her again.*)

LAURA

How can you think such a thing?

TOM

You sent me away . . . you . . . Anyway, when you heard this morning it must have made you sick.

LAURA

(*Sits on edge of bed*)
Tom, I'm going to tell you something. (TOM *won't turn*) Tom? (*He still won't turn*) It was the nicest kiss I've ever had . . . from anybody. (TOM *slowly turns and looks at her*) Tom, I came up to say good-bye. (TOM *shakes his head, look-*

ing at her) I'm going away . . . I'll probably never see you again. I'm leaving Bill. (TOM *knits his brows questioning*) For a lot of reasons . . . one of them, what he's done to you. But before I left, I wanted you to know, for your own comfort, you're more of a man now than he ever was or will be. And one day you'll meet a girl, and it will be right. (TOM *turns away in disbelief*) Tom, believe me.

TOM

I wish I could. But a person knows . . . knows inside. Jesus, do you think after last night I'd ever . . . (*He stops. After a moment, he smiles at her*) But thanks . . . thanks a lot. (*He closes his eyes. LAURA looks at him a long time. Her face shows the great compassion and tenderness she feels for this miserable boy. After some time, she gets up and goes out the door. A moment later she appears in the hall door. She pauses for a moment, then reaches out and closes it, and stays inside.*

TOM, *when he hears the door close, his eyes open. He sees she has left his bedroom. Then in complete misery, he lies down on the bed, like a wounded animal, his head at the foot of the bed.*

LAURA *in a few moments appears in the bedroom doorway. She stands there, and then comes in, always looking at the slender figure of the boy on the bed. She closes the bedroom door.*

TOM *hears the sound and looks around. When he sees she has come back, he turns around slowly, wonderingly, and lies on his back, watching her.*

LAURA *seeing a bolt on the door, slides it to. Then she stands looking at TOM, her hand at her neck. With a slight and delicate movement, she unbuttons the top button of her blouse, and moves towards* TOM. *When she gets alongside the bed, she reaches out her hand, still keeping one hand at her blouse.* TOM *makes no move. Just watches her.*

LAURA *makes a little move with the outstretched hand, asking for his hand.* TOM *slowly moves his hand to hers.*)

LAURA

(*Stands there holding his hand and smiling gently at him. Then she sits and looks down at the boy, and after a moment, barely audible*)
And now . . . nothing?
(TOM's *other hand comes up and with both his hands he brings her hand to his lips.*)

LAURA

(*Smiles tenderly at this gesture, and after a moment*)
Years from now . . . when you talk about this . . . and you will . . . be kind.
(*Gently she brings the boy's hands toward her opened blouse, as the lights slowly dim out . . . and . . .*

THE CURTAIN FALLS

THE END

price 2.75
Santa Claus

a man
play directly - knowing
2 people unhesitantly
give all assuredly
has experienced
these things

1/2 help your
friends